The Winemaker

MAINE MORNINGS BOOK 1

Michelle MacQueen

Ann Maree Craven

ANN MAREE CRAVEN
MICHELLE MACQUEEN

Editing by Caitlin Haines
Cover by Melissa A Craven at Bookly Style

Chapter One

LENA

There was something magical about the bay at twilight. Not the pixie dust and fairy wings kind of magic, the imaginary kind that left a person wishing for something they couldn't have.

No, this kind of power was very much here, very much within reach. It was a quiet that came over the water after the boats were tucked into the marina and everyone who normally filled the air with their chatter along the boardwalk had gone home.

Some people said I had my head in the clouds, that Selena Contreras would never achieve anything extraordinary. Maybe they were right, but tonight I wished for so many things as I lay in the clearing beyond the trees. Beyond the confines of the traditions that dictated what my life would be before I was even born.

But living along the beautiful Maine coastline made me feel like anything was possible.

I'd ridden my moped from my family's orchard down dusty back roads and through town to get to my favorite spot near the bay boardwalk.

I stared up into the darkening sky. Soon, I wouldn't be able to see anything save the sweeping beam of the distant lighthouse that turned the dull, gray rocks silver.

A sigh rattled from my lungs as I let my body relax into the ground, releasing the strain of another day's work. I loved my family's orchard. Some days, I didn't even mind working my hands to the bone to keep it going. We could only afford minimal help, and it was on the entire family to pitch in, even grandma, though I think she enjoyed it the most.

But other days—days when all I felt was a bone-weary ache in my soul—on those days, I wanted something more.

As stars began dotting the sky, I listened to the sound of the gentle waves rushing up against the rocks. There weren't big waves this far into the inlet that led to our little town of Superiore Bay, but as the wind rippled over the surface, it created a tiny splashing that was comforting in its rhythm.

The purr of a boat engine nearing the shore had me lifting my head. I recognized that sound. It came from a tiny fishing boat, the only one that would dare venture near the rocks this late in the day when shadows cloaked the shore.

Because it was driven by someone who never thought anything would happen to him. Carter Ashford. My best friend. A best friend I wasn't allowed to have.

I pushed to my feet, throwing my dark wavy hair over my shoulders before shoving my hands into the pockets of my overalls.

The boat ran up onto the only gap in the rocks, a tiny strip of beach Carter and I found years ago, barely large enough for a boat. It was the only place we could see each other without our families hearing of it.

The Cont rerases and the Ashfords were rivals. We lived on opposite sides of the bay, them in their mansion on the edge of their vineyard and us in our run-down Victorian-style house among the orchards we put our blood sweat and tears into for generations. Grapes verses apples, but the rivalry ran deeper than fruit, though all I knew was the feud dated back several generations before us.

Older people could be so childish.

Carter hopped out of his boat, dragging it farther onto the beach before climbing up the rocks to the grassy area where I waited. The boardwalk sat behind us, dozens of feet above the rocks and boulders that concealed us from the prying eyes of the town.

His wide, boyish grin made it hard to keep a stern face, but I did my best.

His smile fell only the slightest bit. "Whoa, who died?"

I took my hands out of my pockets and crossed my arms. "You do realize it's getting dark, yes?"

He blew auburn curls out of his face. "I'll be fine, Lena." He threw himself onto the ground with a roll of his eyes.

It wasn't the first time we'd had this conversation. I sat beside him. "You could get seriously hurt taking your boat out at this time of day. It's going to be completely dark when you head home." Only experienced boaters went out at night around here, and few came near the rocks, preferring the well-lit marina instead.

He shrugged, his nonchalance irritating. "I'll be fine," he said again and nudged me. "You worry too much."

I drew my knees up to my chest. "And you don't worry enough."

His smile widened, and I wanted to smack it off his face, but instead, I found myself returning the expression. Carter and I had been friends ever since the first day of the second grade. Over the years, various people from our parents and brothers to random nosy townspeople had many "talks" with us about how it wasn't appropriate for us to be friends.

It wasn't like I was going to marry the guy. Carter was basically my brother. Not to mention he was an Ashford. As much as I loved him, I could never join that toxic family.

Carter threw an arm around me and pulled me into a side hug. "What else was I supposed to do to see my favorite girl? I couldn't very well drive."

The road to our spot led right past the boardwalk shops, and Carter's Ferrari wasn't exactly unrecognizable.

I sighed, leaning into him. "I just don't want anything happening to you." I had very few friends in my life, in part because most people in this town bowed down to the Ashfords who practically owned the very roads they drove on. And then, there was the fact I spent all my free time working for my family. Not exactly the kind of girl people wanted to be friends with.

Except for Carter, I'd only ever had one close friend. And she left years ago, and was never coming back.

"You seem tired, Lena." He pulled back to look at me in the way only he did, like he could tell exactly what was going on in my head. I swore, in another life, we were twins separated at birth.

"I'm tired." It was a particularly long week. I'd worked all day every day and then spent the evenings on my own plans. Plans my family would never approve.

I got to my knees and crawled over to my little yellow moped. It wasn't exactly a Ferrari, but it got me where I needed to go. I reached into the bag hanging off the back and pulled out a roll of papers.

Returning to Carter, I flattened them on the ground. He pulled out his phone to use as a flashlight, leaning down to look at my drawings. "You did these?"

I nodded, nibbling on my lower lip. He was the only person who knew how far into the project I was. My parents still thought it was an abstract idea I'd never actually follow through with.

When my grandfather died, he left me his half of the orchard without telling anyone ahead of time. I'd never known why he didn't give it to my grandma, but now I was an equal partner with my dad, something he still couldn't wrap his head around.

I thought it was time for us to stop barely getting by and make an effort to improve our business. To diversify our income before it dried up completely.

Carter flipped through the pages, my drawings of the complex I wanted to build. A cider tasting room. A general store to sell apples and apple-like things. And so much more.

"You added a restaurant?" He rubbed his fingers over the stubble that was a constant on his unshaven face. He'd never been one to grow a full beard, but he also wasn't all about the extra personal grooming.

It made him look less like a fancy Ashford, and I liked that about him.

His eyes lifted to mine in the dark, and I knew exactly how they appeared. Gray. Intelligent.

Some days, I really wanted to love this man. I mean, I did, but not like *that*. I wished he gave me butterflies, the kind I'd never felt before. Even though it would be way too complicated if he did.

"I thought there could be a cafe where we'd serve apple dumplings, hot cider, and the like. Then, a more formal sitting room where people could get fancier dishes like apple braised pork."

"It's genius."

"You think so?" Any time I talked about this dream with my family, they nodded along as if they understood, but they didn't. Not really.

"Lena, the town needs something like this to bring in tourism year round."

A smile spread slowly across my lips. "My thoughts exactly."

He continued looking at the drawings, flipping back and forth between them. "Have you shown this to your dad?"

I snorted out a laugh. "Because that would go over so well."

"Give the man some credit. He loves you." Carter was forever lecturing me about my dad. He didn't really know him since he wasn't allowed at the house, but from what he'd told me, his relationship with his own father was a lot rockier than mine. *The Ashford*, as people tended to call the patriarch of Carter's family, was a force to be reckoned with.

My dad might not believe in this idea, but his didn't believe in *him*.

I rolled the papers up and stuffed them back in the bag before returning and lying back on the grassy slope. Carter rested beside me, his face lifted to the sky.

A cool wind ruffled through the trees, and I breathed in the fresh, salty air. There was nothing like late spring or summer in Superiore Bay, no comparison. It was only May, but during the day, I could already feel the summer heat.

"Do you remember the summers in high school?" he asked suddenly.

I turned my head to look at him, knowing exactly where this was headed. Harper. The girl neither of us quite got over. She'd spent her summers here, and Carter had loved her. Me … well, she was the best female friend I'd ever had, maybe the only true one.

And she'd left us eight years ago and never came back.

I reached over and threaded my fingers through his. "We've got us." It was what we said whenever anything got real in other parts of our lives. When we felt stuck in a cycle we couldn't break free of, stuck in lives we didn't want, we had us. When other people broke our hearts, we had us.

"You realize we're like the Romeo and Juliet of best friends, right?"

I couldn't help laughing at his comparison. "Just please don't die for me."

He squeezed my hand. "I wish we didn't always have to hide."

I knew exactly how he felt. Having Carter in my life was like having a secret lover without the physical aspects. It was like keeping the most important relationship I had from the other people I loved.

I scooted closer and rested my head on his chest, listening to the steady beat of his heart. No one else would ever understand. They wouldn't get that while we loved each other deeply, we weren't *in* love.

There were other kinds of closeness. And one day, when I did fall in love, that person would have to let Carter keep a part of me, the best friend part. We were soul mates.

"You and I, Lena, we're more than they say we are."

I hummed in agreement, trying to keep my eyes open.

He went on. "Our fathers will see that one day. My brother …" He sighed.

I lifted my head. "What did Conner do now?"

Conner Ashford was the second oldest Ashford sibling, the second of three boys and one girl. He was also kind of a jerk.

"Nothing, it's just … he saw me leaving tonight and interrogated me."

"That's nothing new."

"No, but I got so frustrated with him I didn't hide the direction I went in."

"So, Conner knows you're here."

"He probably assumes."

"Will he tell your father?" I asked.

He was quiet for a moment. "I never know what he'll do."

Car tires coming up the dirt road had me jerking up. "You have to go."

Carter didn't have to be told twice. "Love you, Lena."

"Love you too." I pushed him toward the rocks.

He jumped over and ran his boat out into the water. I heard the engine start up and prayed he'd make it back to Ashford Estates safely.

A beat up red pickup truck stopped next to my moped, and the door opened. I waited for my dad to step out and tell me he'd seen Carter here, but instead, a smaller foot reached for the ground. My grandma hopped out with surprising agility.

She walked through the dark to approach me, her arms crossed. "*Mija*, I've been sent to find you for dinner." I loved my grandma, but I was an adult, and my entire family treated me like I was still a teenager. Sure, I didn't have to live in the main house anymore, instead living in the converted old bunk house my brother and I fixed up, but I was still expected for dinner, even when that dinner came very late.

"I was just out here … thinking."

She chuckled softly. "And I'm sure that Ashford boy helps with that."

"Gram …" My steps faltered. "Are you going to tell Dad?"

She studied me for a moment. "Your father has a lot on his mind. He doesn't need to know everything." She winked. Winked! I loved this woman.

I surprised her with a hug. "Thank you." If my dad found out I was still spending time with Carter, he'd find a way to put an end to it. And sometimes, it felt like Carter was the best part of my life.

How sad was that? Our families hated each other. We were from different worlds. There were absolutely no romantic feelings between us. Yet, the thought of losing him stole the breath from my lungs.

Grandma shoved me away from her with a laugh. "Get that bike of yours in the truck."

"It's a moped, not a bike."

She ignored my correction. "We need to get back to the house before Enzo eats all our dinner."

I hauled the moped into the truck bed and climbed in next to her, feeling lighter than I had when I first sought an escape out here with Carter.

It was that magic.

The magic of the bay at dusk.

Chapter Two

CONNER

"What do you expect from me, Dad? Carter's a grown man, he can do whatever he wants."

My father turned his critical gaze on me. I knew what that look meant. I'd been on the receiving end of it my entire life. It was his 'do as you're told' look, but I outgrew that demand at least a decade ago.

My younger brother, Carter, not so much. The little coward was hiding somewhere, avoiding another lecture from Dad.

"You are my heir, Conner, and the Ashford legacy will be yours to command one day when I'm gone. You need to keep your brothers in line. Keep Carter away from that Contreras girl. The last thing we need is for him to get it in his head to marry that girl—or worse, get her pregnant."

I smiled at the thought of a Contreras-Ashford wedding. "He'd do it just to tick you off." I shuffled through the pile of paperwork on my desk, avoiding my father's icy gray gaze. He was right. The Ashford empire was mine to run—whether I wanted it or not. Most days I did. The winery was in my blood. The contracts, employees, and the incredible responsibility of it all.

"Keep your mind on the business, son. You spend too much time with your hybrid crops and that mangy dog of yours and not nearly enough on what matters."

I absently reached down to scratch between Duke's ears. He was *not* mangy. He was a regal brindled Irish wolfhound with wiry gray, brown, and black fur. About seven feet tall when he stood on his hind legs, and the most loyal dog in the world. He was my best friend. Pathetic. But it was true.

"Sure thing, Dad. I'll talk to Carter about his ... associations." *And then, I'll watch it go in one ear and out the other.*

"See that you do." My father stood, his back ramrod straight. "I don't have the patience for Carter's rebellions anymore. I don't know if that boy will ever grow up."

"He will, Dad. He just needs to find his own path." The more Dad came down on Carter, the more Carter pushed back. If they would just stop trying to make each other crazy, my life would certainly improve.

My father turned back at the door, scowling at my choice of office space. "And some boys just need a kick in the pants and a little old school discipline to get through to them."

"We're not cutting him off, Dad. Carter's not a bad kid." We'd had this discussion before. Dad thought it would do his youngest some good to have to make his own way without the support of his ample trust fund. I had more confidence in my brother. Carter would figure out his way soon enough.

"Yeah, well, he's not a kid anymore either." My father stepped out of the barn where I kept my office and left me to my piles of paperwork.

After college, when I first started working for Ashford Winery, I worked in the fancy offices in town with my father full time. Since then, as I took on more responsibility, I made it clear I couldn't tolerate the stuffy executive's corner suite in town more than necessary. I only worked there part time. For the rest, the barn right here on the Ashford Estate suited me just fine. I preferred being closer to the vineyards and our workers. I'd also divided the traditional barn space into two sections. The front was my wide-open office space, and the rear of the barn was outfitted with vintage equipment for my winemaking experimentations.

It had taken a long time to get my father to understand I wanted to be more hands on in the family business. I wanted to be approachable in ways my father and grandfather before me hadn't been.

"You can come out now," I called into the shadows at the back of the barn. "He's gone."

"How'd you know I was here?" Carter shuffled toward my desk, his hands shoved deep into his jeans pockets.

"I heard you come in through the back just before Dad came storming in the front. He saw you leaving the bay boardwalk earlier. And we all know you weren't there for the shopping."

"Who says I don't like shopping?" Carter toed his boot through the fresh hay I'd just laid out in the stalls for Duke.

"Says everyone who ever met you, Carter." I looked up with a grin I couldn't hide. My little brother was many things, but complicated wasn't one of them.

"I buy things." Carter dropped into the chair in front of my desk wearing his patented cheeky smile, his too long auburn curls bouncing around his face. I envied his laid back life.

"If it can be ordered from the internet, yes." I returned to my desk. I needed to finish going through several new purchasing contracts before I could call it a day. "But if it requires you actually stepping into a store—especially the fancy boutiques at the bay boardwalk—it's not going to happen. So, you were with her again. At your little hiding spot under the boardwalk." I hated the tone of accusation that entered my voice. I wasn't Carter's father. I was barely his employer, but I'd really rather just be his brother.

"So what if I was?" Carter rolled his eyes. "The Contrerases are good people, and Selena is my best friend."

"You know how our family feels about those people." I winced at how awful that sounded. Like the Contrerases weren't good enough for the Ashfords.

"Congratulations, brother, you've never sounded more like Dad. He'd be so proud. We should call him back and have you reenact that little moment there."

"I'm trying to help you." I sighed. He was right, I sounded like a jerk to my own ears.

"They aren't the enemy." Carter moved to the edge of his seat. "This whole family feud is a little too Capulets and Montagues, don't you think?"

More like the Hatfield and McCoys. I gave a mental shrug. The kid was right. The bad blood between the families was old news. I couldn't even begin to explain how it all came about. But keeping Carter away from the Contreras girl would make my life easier, and I was all about making my life easier.

"Hey, Duke." Carter grinned as Duke emerged from under my desk. The traitor loved my brother. "You're looking as handsome and as tall as ever."

Duke was enormous—a gentle giant for sure. He busied himself sniffing Carter's hair, and since they were at eye level, it made for a strange sight. "I think he likes my cologne."

"Duke, enough, go get your teddy." I pointed to the large bed in the nearest stall where Duke took his afternoon naps. The great gray beast scampered over like a young pup and snatched up his "teddy," a toddler-sized golden teddy bear he'd had since he was a baby. The eyes were chewed out, and I'd had to stitch it back together more times than I could count. I didn't know what I'd do if anything ever happened to teddy. Duke would be inconsolable.

"One of these days, I'm going to dog-nap this guy." Carter shook his head, smiling at Duke's antics with teddy.

"Trust me, you'd call begging for me to come get him." I shoved the contracts to the corner of my desk. They could wait until tomorrow. "Just ... stay away from the girl. It's not worth the hassle."

"Says the guy with no friends." Carter glanced up from watching Duke. "You'd sing a different tune if you had a best friend you couldn't live without."

"You really expect me to believe you're just friends with this girl?" I sat back against my chair, studying my brother's face for any sign that he might be lying. I'd known her as long as him, though not nearly as well. She was pretty, and my brother was a sucker for a pretty girl. Especially one that would make our father crazy with rage.

"I don't expect anything from you. Just stay out of my business, and we're good." Carter leaned forward just as the phone rang. "You can tell Dad we had the talk, and I'll behave myself long enough to get him off your back. And mine."

I nodded as I reached for the phone. I could live with that arrangement for the time being.

"Conner Ashford," I answered the phone, waving to my little brother as he headed out the door to an evening free of responsibility. I envied his ability to walk away sometimes. Well, most of the time.

"What can I do for you, Eli?" I'd hoped to be out of the office at a reasonable time tonight, but with a late call from the family lawyer, who was also my cousin, it didn't look like that was going to happen.

"Conner, glad I caught you, there's been a development on the parcel of land you were hoping to sell."

"You have a buyer?" I ran a hand through my hair. It would be good news if Eli had an interested buyer—not that I needed the money. The land was fairly useless to me now. Ever since the Bay Yacht Club acquired the beach front parcel right next to the Ashford property, any plans to develop it had gone on the back burner. Better to let some other developer come in and put up affordable housing or some other less profitable project that would be a waste of my time. It was good land, I just didn't need it.

"Yes," Eli hedged. "Maybe … it depends."

I sighed as I sat down at my desk. "Just get to the point. I'm sure you're as anxious to get home as I am." Not that I had anyone to go home to. It was just me and Duke … and the grapes here at Ashford Winery … unless I wanted to spend the evening with Dad and my grandfather, which I did not.

"Someone's interested. She hasn't put in an official offer yet, but she's eager. I'm not sure she can scrape together the full market value, but she means to make a decent offer."

"Good news, Eli. I don't care if she can't come up to full market value. I just want to be rid of the parcel." And continuing to pay the high property taxes on a useless piece of land was just a bad business decision. "Who's the buyer?" I grabbed a pen to scribble down the name so I could reach out to her realtor and get the ball rolling.

"That's the thing." I could hear the hesitation in Eli's voice. "I need you to keep an open mind here. It's Selena Contreras."

"Are you serious? What do the Contrerases want with more property? They can barely handle the taxes on their lands as it is." Really, it was only a matter of time before Orchard Hill Farm belonged to the Ashfords.

The winery was a big tourist draw. So was the quaint little beach town. But Orchard Hill Farm was also responsible for bringing in tourists during their harvest season. And for the last several years, they'd experienced a disappointing harvest. What could this girl be thinking? Now was a time to trim back the excess and reevaluate her business plans for the future. It was not time to charge forward, buying expensive property she couldn't afford to do anything with.

"She has plans," Eli said. "Big plans, but that's all I'm at liberty to say."

If it were just up to me, I wouldn't care one way or the other if Selena Contreras decided to buy all the land for sale in Superiore Bay. But it wasn't just up to me. My father would have to agree to sell the land, and he would never sell a blade of grass to a member of the Contreras family.

Chapter Three

LENA

Whenever I went into town with my brother, people tended to stare. Not at me. I was around town a lot, but Enzo rarely got involved in town affairs. A year younger than me, he was also more emotionally invested in the orchard. One day, I hoped he'd be able to take over the running of it while I had my own business.

A business that had brought me to town.

But his aloofness wasn't the only reason the people we'd known all our lives stared. My brother was beautiful, at least according to the little old ladies who fueled the gossip magazine in town, the *Weekly Wine*. Gag me at the name. Did everything in this town have to be about the Ashfords and their perfect wine?

The magazine had a section called "sightings" where they chronicled where they saw all the town's golden boys. This included Enzo, Conner Ashford—ugh—a few cops, firefighters, the mayor, and several others.

The old ladies lusted after them. It was kind of funny, actually.

With his tanned skin, cerulean eyes, and broad muscles

built through hard work rather than working out, I'd had to put up with a lot of swooning no sister should ever have to see.

I yelped as Enzo grabbed my arm and yanked me toward the alcove in front of the door to Hugga Mugga, the one and only coffee shop in town.

"Ow, let go. What's wrong with you?"

Enzo looked behind us and sighed. "Mrs. Peterson was coming our way."

One corner of my mouth curled up. "Your girlfriend?"

He groaned. Mrs. Mary Peterson was about seventy and had a habit of saying inappropriate things. I kind of loved her.

"If you're going to make me hide, the least you can do is buy me a coffee." I pushed open the glass door that showcased the bright and bubbly Hugga Mugga logo. The name was as cheesy as our town.

Inside, the place was packed with morning patrons getting their injections of caffeine. I wasn't much of a coffee drinker, but this place made killer scones.

"I'm getting breakfast too."

Enzo rolled his eyes. "And I guess I'm paying for that as well?"

I linked my arm with his. "You're such a good brother."

We'd always been close, closer than close. As this town was one to take sides in any dispute as though it was the local sport, it was usually the Contreras kids against the world.

Inside, the coffee shop was warm, with dark wooden floors and sky blue walls. I'd always loved it here. Shelby Yin stood behind the counter, looking bored. Her inky black hair was piled high on her head, and pink glasses perched on her nose. I almost asked why she was here and not in school, but then I remembered they had the day off for some teacher training thing. I'd read about it in the *Weekly Wine* that annoyed me so much. Sue me, I was a customer.

I really needed to get out more.

"What can I get you?" she asked in a monotone voice.

Enzo and I ordered iced mochas and cranberry-orange scones. He paid, and we ducked out into the early morning sun. I checked the time on my phone and realized I'd be a bit early to my meeting with the lawyer.

My brother didn't know why I wanted to come to town, but he'd been dying to get out. He had a few errands to run while I had my meeting, and he hadn't asked questions. He was good like that.

We headed across the street toward the town square and didn't see them until it was too late. Sitting in a row of chairs near the small gazebo was the gossip posse. That was what Carter and I called them. We'd avoided Mrs. Peterson before, but here she was again, and they'd already seen us.

"Selena!" Mrs. Jeffries called. "Selena, come here and bring that brother of yours with you."

I tugged him with me, not wanting to be rude.

Along with Mrs. Peterson and Mrs. Jeffries was Mrs. Chapman, my favorite of the bunch. Carter and I had spent a lot of time at her house when her granddaughter Harper Chapman visited in the summers.

Mrs. Chapman gave us a warm smile. "It's been a while since I saw one Contreras, let alone two. How are you, dears?"

I returned her smile. "Good, thank you." I elbowed Enzo.

He cleared his throat. "Fine, fine."

"Yes, you are." Mrs. Peterson's gaze slid up the length of him, and he fidgeted beside me.

Feeling bad for him, I tried to shift the attention to me. "Have you heard from Harper recently, Mrs. Chapman?"

She smiled at the mention of her successful granddaughter. "She called me just last night. She's married, you know." I did know that. We were still friends on social media. "And a reporter for the *Boston Globe*! I'm so proud of that girl."

I was proud of my old friend too. She achieved the dreams

she used to talk about. I just wish she hadn't had to leave me and Carter behind to do it. Stifling those thoughts, I kept my smile bright. It was all I could do.

Mrs. Jeffries met my gaze. "What about you, Selena? Any prospective husbands on the horizon?"

Enzo coughed out a laugh, and I "accidentally" stepped on his foot, my smile never wavering. "I'm just focused on my family's business."

"You won't be young forever, dear. Eventually, those Contreras good looks you both have will turn into this." She gestured to the three of them.

I shook my head. "I would be lucky to age like you beauties."

That made her laugh. "You two were always charmers. Tell you what, I have a grandson who lives about an hour from here. That's not too far, is it?"

It wasn't the first time I'd heard about this grandson.

Mrs. Peterson scoffed. "She doesn't want to marry Hank, Anita. He only graduated high school last year."

Mrs. Jeffries looked offended, but it was the truth. I wasn't going to date an eighteen-year-old kid.

"Plus," Mrs. Peterson continued, "Glen is more her type."

I wasn't sure what they thought my type was, but it definitely wasn't a man ten years my senior who lived with his parents and worked part time, spending the rest of his time playing video games.

"Oh, hey," Enzo said suddenly. "There's Harrison. I need to have a word with him." I lifted my eyes to where Harrison Ashford walked down the brick path crisscrossing the wide-open green spaces that made up the square.

I wanted to murder my brother as he jogged toward the only Ashford he put up with. Harrison was the mayor of Superiore Bay, so we didn't really have a choice but to deal with him, but he was also different from his Ashford Estate cousins.

I turned my attention back to the ladies in front of me, my

eyes catching on the paper in Mrs. Chapman's hands. "Is that a new issue of the *Weekly Wine?*"

"Sure is, honey. I'm done with it if you'd like to see it."

"Thank you." I took it from her. "I must be on my way. I have a meeting this morning."

After waving goodbye, I headed toward the row of shops along the Boulevard, which was what we called the main drag around the square.

I didn't have time to read much of the gossip before stepping into Bath Babes, my favorite shop. It was owned by an elderly woman named Candice Fletcher. I didn't know her well, but the store sold my favorite candles.

The bell above the bright yellow door chimed as I stepped inside, and I was immediately assaulted with a tantalizing combination of scents from the section of candles to my right. This place sold everything homemade. Candles, soaps, environmentally friendly cleaners.

I knew after my meeting with the lawyer I was going to need my favorite calming scent. It was a candle they simply called "Relax," a mix of vanilla, chamomile flowers, and mint.

I didn't talk to the other patrons. Other than the gossip posse, most of them didn't speak to me. That would require betraying their Ashford overlords.

Mrs. Fletcher smiled at me as I walked toward the counter with the candle, but then, she smiled at everyone. I wasn't sure I'd ever met anyone else who was quite as nice as her.

"You do love these, don't you?" She laughed.

I went through a lot of candles. "Nothing else can calm me down quite so quickly."

"You're wound a little tight, Lena." She reached for a basket of bath bombs on the counter. "I'm going to throw one of these in. Try it. I promise, it'll be the best thing you've ever done for yourself. A little self-care."

I wasn't really one for self-care, or bubble baths, but I smiled in thanks.

Looping my bag over one arm, I left the shop. As I walked, I opened up the copy of the *Weekly Wine* Mrs. Chapman had given me.

It was mostly the usual gossip. Old Mr. Franklin, who manned the lighthouse at Superiore Point, was apparently dating a woman from Hidden Cove—a treasonous betrayal to most of Superiore Bay. My eyes scanned the gossip, some of it making me chuckle. Had Matt Davidson really streaked through the town square two nights ago?

It was probably a celebration for one of the high school sports teams busy wrapping up their season.

When I got to the sightings section, I nearly stopped breathing.

Sighted: Carter Ashford, motoring across the inlet to meet with Selena Contreras. Will we have a joining of the two rival families?

Oh no. I was lucky my parents didn't read this stuff, but someone in Carter's family likely did, and the news would get to his father, a man who terrified me.

I looked up just in time to see Conner Ashford walking toward me and ducked into the nearest doorway. Maybe he hadn't seen me. But now, I had a problem. I couldn't go back out there and walk to the lawyer's office. Not without running into Conner.

I glanced at the door I stood in front of. The Rusty Spoon. Perfect. Pulling out my phone, I dialed the lawyer's personal cell. I'd known him most of my life and rarely called his office. He was an old friend of my brother's but also another Ashford cousin.

"Lena, aren't you supposed to be in my office right about now?"

"Hey, Eli." I leaned back against the brick next to the door. "Change of plans. Think you can meet me at the diner?"

Most people would say no during the work day, but Eli only laughed. "Which of my cousins are you avoiding?"

Eli knew my family too well. "Conner."

"Well, you're lucky I'm hungry. You're buying me breakfast."

"Yeah, sure. I'm already here. See you soon." I hung up and slid my phone into my purse, taking my eyes off the sidewalk just long enough to miss someone walking up to me.

I sensed him as one sensed a predator and lifted my eyes slowly, my breath catching in my throat.

There, standing in front of me was my least favorite person in this tiny little town. Conner Ashford was powerful, dangerous, but no matter how much his eyes hardened when he looked at me, I refused to be scared of him.

I refused to bow down and kiss his feet like everyone else did.

And I was sure he hated me for it.

Chapter Four

CONNER

Selena Contreras. I wasn't sure what it was about her that set me so on edge. After running into her brother when I went to meet my cousin, I wasn't in the mood to deal with another Contreras.

But this girl, with her smug flaunting of the generations old rules dictating our families stay apart, rubbed me the wrong way. Even now, disgust rolled across her face when she looked at me. Disgust I was certain she didn't show Carter.

"Did you want something?" she asked, her chin lifting and her deep brown eyes meeting mine. Long lashes brushed her cheeks, and I steeled myself, knowing how the dark-haired girl could worm her way into men's hearts. Just like my brother.

I'd never believed him when he said he wasn't in love with her.

"Are you here for your meeting with Eli?" They were the wrong words with the wrong tone, but I couldn't keep the taunting note from my voice.

"How ..." She shook her head. "Is that any of your business?"

"It is when it's my land you're trying to purchase." My father had already said no to selling to a Contreras. It hadn't been my choice. For a reason I couldn't explain, I wanted her to think I'd personally thwarted her plans. I was probably saving her family from ruin. She'd bankrupt them if she got the loans she sought.

"Your ..." Her words sputtered before she tensed. "I didn't know it was your land."

"And if you had known?" I wanted her to say it, to admit she'd have walked away from all her grand plans just so she never paid the Ashfords a dime.

But she didn't.

"Who I buy the land from doesn't matter." She crossed her arms over her chest, her eyes glittering with defiance.

"Your plans will never succeed." She wasn't a business-woman. No one in her family since her grandfather had a real head for business. It was why they struggled so much.

"My plans—"

"Your boyfriend told me."

"My boy—Carter."

She didn't dispute my characterization of him, but something I couldn't understand flashed in her eyes. Betrayal, maybe. Or sadness. Whatever it was, I suddenly felt bad for everything I'd said. But it was too late now.

"You listen to me, Conner." She stepped forward, pushing me back toward the crowd of onlookers who'd stopped to watch two pillars of the town knock each other down. "You don't get to decide if I succeed or fail."

"That's an expensive piece of land, Selena Contreras." Her eyes narrowed at my use of her full name, but I didn't stop. "You'll never be able to afford the full market price we're asking for. The Ashfords control what happens in this town."

Her eyes blazed with anger.

"Hit him, girl!" Mrs. Chapman called from the gazebo just

across the street from the Rusty Spoon. "Sock him right in that smug face of his."

I could tell Lena was considering it.

"I really wish he'd meet my granddaughter." I recognized Mrs. Jeffries' voice. She and the other old crones were sitting near the gazebo in the square, sticking their noses in where they didn't belong. How many times did I have to turn down a blind date with that woman's granddaughter?

Lena, seeming to become aware we had an audience, took a step back. "You Ashfords think everything revolves around you." She lifted her voice. "But we are not under your control."

"I'd gladly be under his control," someone said, I wasn't sure who. Others tittered, gathering on the street corner to watch. No one was taking any of this seriously. But it was serious. More than serious.

The Contreras family thought they were on the same footing as the Ashfords, but what it all boiled down to was a small struggling family against the town's benefactors. The Ashfords had a hand in everything that happened here.

My cousin, Harrison, was the mayor. We owned most of the commercial property along the Boulevard. Even my brother, Conrad, was a revered figure with all his work protecting the wild horses at the island sanctuary across the bay.

A presence loomed behind me, and Lena relaxed. I didn't have to look to know it was Enzo, who was both bigger than I was and more willing to get into a fight in front of the entire town.

"Something wrong here, Ashford?" His voice was deep, imposing.

I held up a hand. "Just having a chat with your sister."

"Doesn't look like much of a chat to me." He muscled his way through the crowd to stand at his sister's side. Despite being younger than me, he wasn't someone I wanted to mess with.

Brawling with townies was beneath me.

A few people had their phones out, and I knew photos of this confrontation would end up in that stupid gossip magazine, the one filling the heads in this town with lies.

"This is hot." Mrs. Peterson fanned herself. "Anyone else hot?"

Lena pushed her brother behind her, her eyes narrowing. Her voiced lowered to a hush. "I'd stand down on this, Conner. You don't want to get in my way."

I enjoyed nothing more than getting in her way. I always had, even when we were young.

Lena's fists clenched at her sides, and I saw the explosion coming before it happened. "Carter always tells me you're not as bad as you seem, but he's wrong, isn't he?" She got close, too close, her voice menacing. "You're just like your father."

I felt her words like a punch in the gut, wishing she'd take them back. I didn't want to be my father. Cold and hard and calculating. Was she right?

"What's going on here?"

I closed my eyes for a brief moment and sighed before turning toward the voice of my father. I was late meeting him at the coffee shop to sign the documents I'd just picked up from Eli. He was putting new rules on Carter's trust.

The crowd parted as if they were the Red Sea and my dad had just stuck his staff in the water. Silence descended over them as they watched him walk forward, his face a mask of calm I knew he didn't feel.

"Lena." He nodded politely her way. "Enzo."

"Mr. Ashford." There was venom in her tone. "How nice to see you."

My father grunted before pasting on a smile. "It's been a while. How are your parents?"

The crowd watched with rapt attention, hanging on my

father's every word. To them, he was like the father of the town and could do no wrong.

I knew better. His impeccable suit and tie and perfect silver hair couldn't hide the fact he was a tyrant. Within his own family and within this town.

The envelope in my hand grew heavy with the weight of the secrets it carried. The amount of control this man wanted over his son. I'd managed to talk him down from the more extreme measures, but Carter still wouldn't be happy.

Lena stared at my father, her eyes narrowing. I couldn't blame her for hating him. He'd actively worked to hurt their business, despite my protestations that we should focus only on our own.

"Let's just go, Lena," Enzo said.

She shook her head. "Eli will be here soon."

"Why are you meeting with Eli?" he whispered, ignoring us. "Is this a date?"

Something clenched inside me at that. I couldn't see Lena and Eli together. I told myself it was because my brother undoubtedly had feelings for her, not because I secretly respected the strength in her gaze, how she didn't cower when confronted by my father.

Not like I did.

"I'll explain inside." She grabbed his arm, yanking him into the diner without another glance for us.

I exhaled slowly and turned to where my dad was glaring at the crowd until they dissipated. He crooked one finger my way. "You, come with me."

We'd made it halfway to the coffee shop before he spoke. "I don't want you to be seen talking to them again."

"You think I planned that?" I couldn't believe him.

"I think you caused a spectacle."

"Dad, our family is always a spectacle. I was just telling her we wouldn't sell the land to her."

He shot me an icy look out of the corner of his eye. "Let Eli handle that. It isn't your job."

"I still think we should have just sold to them and been done with it." I would never understand this family feud, even if I played into it. It went back many generations, and it wasn't only the Ashfords playing dirty. I saw the way Lena's parents looked at me and my brothers. I'd heard the things people said. That we were spoiled rich kids who didn't respect anything we had.

I might be an Ashford, but that didn't mean I didn't work hard or that the pressure of being a part of this family wasn't just as intense as it was to be a part of theirs.

"You picked up the documents?"

I held up the manila envelope. "Everything you need to control your youngest son." I couldn't keep the disapproval out of my voice.

My father ignored it. As always. He didn't care what I really thought, only that I obeyed.

Exhaustion suddenly came over me. Maybe I'd feel better if Lena had listened to old Mrs. Chapman and punched me. Then, I could truly despise her, instead of this unwanted admiration.

We entered the coffee shop, a cutesy name I refused to utter, and Dad made the rounds, saying hello to everyone he could. He was a popular man, a revered man.

And I, by extension, was Superiore Bay royalty as well.

Even if it wasn't a crown I wanted.

I was much happier at the vineyard with my dog and my grapes. But there were expectations that came with being an Ashford.

I grabbed a copy of the *Weekly Wine* from the rack and found an open table. My father sat across from me as we waited. He didn't order coffee at the counter. The people who worked here brought it to us. And if I tried to get it myself, he'd only admonish me.

I read through the gossip magazine, looking for any sign of my family. We ended up in these pages a lot, usually in fake stories submitted by anonymous sources.

Today, only Carter's name appeared. I scoffed at the idea that Carter or any Ashford would ever marry a Contreras. Even if she wasn't infuriating, my father would never allow it. But it seemed he wasn't the only one who knew Carter went to meet Lena. For the first time, I wondered how he always knew these things. Did he have spies all over town?

That seemed a little extreme, but I wouldn't put it past him.

As I thought of my youngest brother, I wondered what it must be like to have that freedom. The freedom to ignore the family rules. The freedom to do whatever he pleased.

And what about Lena? Carter had a friend he was willing to face punishment for, to risk losing everything for. He refused to give her up, and I couldn't help feeling the tiniest bit jealous.

Chapter Five

LENA

"The Ashfords think they own this town." I slumped into a booth at the Rusty Spoon, my brother sliding in across from me.

Enzo picked up a menu. "They kind of do."

"That's beside the point." I didn't care if they owned most of the commercial property in town. It didn't mean they owned us. Sure, their winery thrived while our orchard barely got by, but that was going to change.

I was going to change it.

"Why are we meeting with Eli anyway? You never answered me about that."

I snatched the menu from him. "*We* aren't meeting with him. I am."

"And you're not going to tell me why?"

"I thought you had errands to run."

He leaned back. "I'm not going anywhere."

I'd tried bringing up business proposals with my parents, and it never ended well. They were stuck in the past, thinking the orchard would keep us going as it always had.

It wouldn't. Not without significant changes.

And Enzo was more like them than Grams and me. I think that was why Grandpa left me his shares and not Enzo. He knew I'd do more with them than wait around for the harvest each year.

And I planned to.

The bell chimed as Eli walked in, his gaze finding us immediately. He was the only man I knew who wore a suit, even as spring prepared for summer. Superiore Bay was a laid back town that never cared much about appearances. Well, clothes anyway. The *Weekly Wine* sure cared how people appeared, how they acted.

"Hey, man." Enzo stood and did a weird back-slapping thing with Eli.

"Didn't know you'd be here, Enzo." They both sat.

Enzo shrugged. "Can't let big sis have all the fun."

Eli's smile faded. "Well, I'm not sure this meeting is going to be much fun."

"Uh oh." I groaned. "That doesn't sound good." But I knew what he was going to tell me. Conner had already done the deed.

"I'm sorry, Lena. I wish I had better news. The Ashfords have turned down your offer."

"Turned down what?" Enzo asked.

Eli ignored him. "You made them a legitimate offer, but I get the feeling this isn't about money. They don't want your family owning any of their land."

Kate Simpson, a middle-aged woman who was never far from her job at the diner, walked up. "Can I get you folks anything?"

Yeah, a way to ruin the Ashfords, to make them feel as low as they tried to push us. But, obviously, that wasn't something Kate could get me. "A piece of cherry pie please."

She gave me a strange look. "It's not lunch yet ..."

"Please."

"Okay, dear."

Enzo ordered coffee, but Eli didn't want anything. So much for me buying him breakfast.

When Kate was gone, I looked back at Eli. "What are my options?"

He drummed his fingers on the table and looked at me in that annoying un-Ashford caring way he had. "You could make another offer anonymously."

My brow furrowed. "How exactly?"

"We could set up a shell corporation for your business enterprises. That way, we wouldn't have to list you as an owner." He leaned in. "This is how a lot of businesses and foreign governments—and ours—funnel money to places they don't want people knowing about."

Something about that didn't sit right with me. I knew it was perfectly legal, but here in Superiore Bay, I didn't want to hide what I was doing.

"I'm not sure that's a good idea."

Enzo's eyes bounced from Eli to me. "I'm still missing something."

Eli scooted out of the booth. "I know we talked about breakfast, but something tells me it's more important for you two to chat. Do you want me to try upping the bid and seeing if, by some miracle, that works?"

"Yeah, let's do that." Not that I could afford any more than my initial offer.

"Raincheck on breakfast?"

"Any time."

He clapped Enzo on the shoulder and sauntered out the way he'd come. There'd been a time I'd crushed hard on Eli, the smooth-talker turned lawyer.

And Enzo knew it.

He narrowed his eyes. "No breakfast dates with my friends."

I sighed, not in the mood for his overprotectiveness, especially when I knew how unfair it was he could be friends with Eli Ashford, but I had to hide my friendship with Carter. The difference between them was, though their fathers were brothers, they had very different views on this town and on us.

Luckily, Kate returned with my pie, and the moment I took a bite, everything looked a little less dreary.

Enzo watched me patiently, waiting for me to explain any of what had just happened. There was no getting out of it.

I swallowed a bite and took a sip of water. "Okay, so, sibling secret?" It was what we said when we didn't want Mom or Dad to know something. Even now, when we were both adults, we kept certain things between us.

"Go on." He nodded with his serene expression, looking much older than the one year my junior he really was.

"So ..." I fiddled with a napkin. "You know the business idea I brought to Dad last year, the one Gramps and I came up with?"

He nodded again.

"I've sort of expanded it." I paused for a reaction, but he was waiting for more. Pulling out my phone, I brought up the pictures I'd taken of my drawings and set the phone on the table.

He picked it up, his eyes squinting as he zoomed in. Minutes ticked by. Hours, days it felt like before he finally looked at me again. "Lena, this is ..." I waited for him to tell me it was too ambitious, that I could never accomplish such an outlandish dream.

But he didn't. Instead, a slow smile spread across his face. "Did you really think the Ashfords would sell to you so you could do this?"

A relieved laugh bubbled out of me. "No. Yes. I was hoping they wouldn't ask Eli who the buyer was."

"Lena, they're businesspeople. They aren't going to sell land like that without vetting everything." He handed me back my phone. "So, we just need to find a different land parcel they don't own."

I shook my head. "It has to be that one."

"Then, we'll make them sell to you. One way or another." The glee in Enzo's eyes should have scared me, but I was just glad he was on my side.

"You don't think I'm nuts, taking on this kind of risk? I could lose my share of the orchard, and that would drive the entire thing under."

"Sis, if we don't do something big, I'm afraid we're going to lose it one day anyway." He stood. "Come on."

My fork was halfway to my mouth. "What? I'm not done with my pie."

"And I promise not to tell Grams you had scones *and* pie for breakfast if you come now."

I groaned and threw some money on the table before following him out.

We'd driven the family pickup to town with its peeling red paint, oversized truck bed, and broken air conditioning. By the time we made it to the dirt roads leading toward home, my hair was in knots from having the windows open.

Mom and Dad weren't at the main house, but we found Grams in the kitchen making lunch. She smiled when she saw us. "My favorite kiddos." I didn't remind her we weren't kids anymore. "How was your morning in town?"

Enzo stole a piece of cucumber she'd been slicing and popped it into his mouth. "Lena punched Conner Ashford."

"Enzo!" I protested.

"Fine, she almost did. I could tell she wanted to. That guy is a piece of work."

Grams gave me a soft smile. "You okay, *mija?*"

"Fine." It wasn't the fight with Conner that had bothered me. Okay, it sort of was. I knew our families were rivals, but I didn't understand why the guy hated me so much. Sure, I was more likely to be seen in overalls and work boots than the designer clothes he wore, but that didn't put me beneath him.

It certainly shouldn't warrant his anger. "What did we ever do to them, Grams?"

"That's a loaded question." Grams carried a plate of chopped veggies and cheese to the table.

"But it's one no one ever gives us an answer to. I know no one wants me to be friends with Carter, but I don't know why. I face Conner's scorn, and there doesn't seem to be an actual reason for it."

Enzo turned in his chair. "If we're ever going to beat them, we need to know what we're actually fighting."

Grams lowered herself into a wooden chair at the table and regarded us. "There is no beating the Ashfords." She sighed. "I should know. I've tried."

I slid into a chair across from her. "You went up against them?"

"It was a long time ago." She suddenly looked very tired.

"Please tell us."

She rubbed a hand across her eyes and chewed on a piece of celery before speaking. "My grandfather, your two times great-grandfather, and his counterpart in the Ashford family were as close as brothers." That was news to me. "It was in a time of much more racism, yet we'd already been in this country for two generations and just tried to blend in."

They still tried to blend in, speaking very little Spanish and observing few cultural experiences. It was kind of sad, if anyone asked me. "You mean an Ashford and a Contreras were allowed to be friends?"

"It was different back then. Our two businesses worked in tandem together. We opened a wine and cider tasting room. It was an odd mingling, but it worked. Those two men built this town into what it is, investing heavily and becoming sort of like the town founders."

Enzo joined us at the table, just as enthralled in our family history as me. "So, what happened?"

Grams looked at each of us in turn. "There was a business deal to bring the two corporations under the same umbrella and grow them from there. The Ashfords had an ample amount of fertile land for us to expand on. It was a business owner's dream the way they worked so well together."

"And?" I leaned in. "Did one of them back out? Swindle the other out of money? Why do we all hate each other now?"

She shook her head. "It was much simpler than that. My uncle Matias, my father's brother, fell in love with an Ashford daughter, Audrey. It was supposed to bring the families closer."

"But it didn't?"

Grams smiled sadly. "No, honey. Matters of the heart are complicated. On the eve of their wedding, Matias took off. He went out west to join the gold rush. I wasn't even born yet when all of this happened, but my father never quite forgave his brother. The Ashfords broke off all business dealings with our family and went out of their way to thwart us for many years."

"They still do," I muttered. How could a love story from so long ago still be haunting the families now? "They're never going to sell to me."

Grams didn't ask what I meant, but I had a feeling she knew everything I was trying to do.

"Whoa." Enzo looked as stunned as I felt. "That's some real book-worthy stuff right there. The dueling families of Superiore Bay."

"It's stupid is what it is." I stood, a sudden and irrational anger burning through me. "No one alive even remembers all of that happening, and yet, here we are still living in the mess they caused. Well, you know what … I don't care. I don't care who our supposed enemies are. I don't care about some tragic love story with people I didn't even know. This feud is ruining everything. And it's time it stopped."

I walked out of the kitchen through the swinging screen door, not stopping until I crossed the yard to the bunkhouse I shared with Enzo. The door slammed shut behind me as my mind worked through every possible solution.

Enzo thought we could find a way to force them into selling to us, but I didn't want that.

I pulled my phone out and stared down at it, knowing I really only had one option. Carter and I once promised not to let our families get between us, that we'd never put each other in a bad position.

But he was my only hope now.

So, I sent him a text.

Lena: Meet me at our spot.

He'd come. He always did. Just like when he needed me, I was there. No matter what our last names were, we had each other's backs.

Chapter Six

CONNER

I watched my brother carefully control his anger, a trait that wasn't exactly known to the Ashfords. But Carter had always been different from my father. Me, I was more like him than I wanted anyone to know.

Carter's jaw ticked, the only sign of his frustration.

Our father, on the other hand, drummed his fingers on the table in agitation. He didn't like Carter's silence or the fact that we'd waited for him for nearly an hour after I was forced to send a text demanding he meet us immediately at Hugga Mugga.

Around us, other patrons had no idea of the power struggle currently happening at this table, the potential for this to be the final straw that made Carter all but abandon us like our brother Conrad had before.

And then there was Jorgina, the youngest of us who'd left for Yale and had yet to return. She was almost a college senior, but none of us knew if she would return to the family fold once she graduated. After Mom died when I was a teenager, I'd vowed to myself I'd never let the family down. I couldn't leave my father and granddad the way my siblings had.

But what about Carter?

His eyes roved the papers I brought from the lawyer. "It's my money." Finally, angry eyes lifted to Dad. Carter wasn't hard, not like the rest of us. Yet, he was stony now, showing no affection, none of the jovial smiles I envied him for.

Dad leaned back in his chair, crossing his arms over his chest. "It is only yours because I allow it to be yours."

Most people with family trusts allowed the recipient to control it once they reached a certain age. Not my father. He'd crafted it for milestones instead. As long as Carter lived the life he did, he could only access a monthly allowance until he turned thirty. And only if he worked for the Ashford empire in some capacity.

Carter scowled, an unfamiliar expression on his face. "So, you're saying I can keep using the money as long as I work?"

"For the family, yes."

"But what about Conrad? He doesn't work for the family."

Conrad was a sore spot for our father. He always had been. Yet, he'd never exerted the pressure over his oldest son like he did the rest of us, and none of us had ever been able to figure out why.

"You listen here, you ungrateful child, Conrad has nothing to do with this."

We all knew what that meant. Dad couldn't touch most of Conrad's money. Carter and Jorgina got the short end of the stick. Because of their ages when Mom died, she'd never had a chance to set up separate trusts for them using her own money. Trusts my father didn't know about until after her accident. Conrad and I had a source of income separate from our father's money, and it drove him insane that he couldn't use it to control us.

"And what if I went and got married tomorrow?" Carter asked, his eyes narrowing. "Then, you couldn't do a thing to stop me from draining the accounts."

Those conditions on his trust … it wasn't only age. His full access began either when he turned thirty or got married. Whichever came first.

There were so many hoops, so many clauses, I could hardly understand most of it.

"So, what?" Carter asked. "You want me to sit in a stuffy office like your clone here?" He gestured to me. Ouch. "Or would you rather I go out into the vineyard and pick grapes?"

I snorted at that, picturing my Ferrari-driving brother doing any sort of manual labor. It showed how little he knew about our own vineyards. Many of our hybrid grapes were picked by machine, and the ones that weren't were delicate and thin skinned. They required special handling, something my father would never trust Carter with.

Carter's phone buzzed, the rattling shaking the table. He snatched it from the surface before I could get a look at the screen, but his lips curled into a tiny smile as he read whatever was there.

I knew that look.

It was reserved for one person.

Selena Contreras.

Carter ignored us and typed away on his phone. I could sense my father's anger coming, and I didn't want to be hit with the shrapnel.

Playing at friends—or something more—with the Contreras girl was like lighting a stick of dynamite in the center of Ashford Estates. Or more accurately, setting off a massive explosion in Superiore Bay, because no one would get through it unscathed.

"Carter." Dad's voice was low, dangerous.

"Hmm?" Carter didn't look up.

"We aren't finished here."

His eyes were no longer hard as he lifted them, his entire posture had relaxed. Not for the first time, I wondered what it would be like to have someone in my life who put me so at ease.

I would inherit Ashford Estates one day, as well as the entire empire we'd built. I'd have more money than I could possibly spend and the prestige that came with it.

Yet, I was jealous of my carefree little brother.

And I wanted to throttle him at the same time. Being an Ashford wasn't about doing what we wanted, it wasn't about being happy.

"Give me your phone." My father held out his hand.

Carter looked to me as if seeking some kind of help, a help I wished I could give him.

But no one went against my father and won. Not even me.

I sighed. "Just do it, Carter."

Betrayal entered his gaze, and I looked away.

He set the phone in our father's hand with a slap. Dad flipped it over and read the screen, red creeping into his cheeks. It was another sign of his anger.

"How many times have we told you to stay away from this girl?" The words were calm, collected, but there was also rage simmering beneath the surface.

"She's not just some girl, Dad." Carter suddenly looked dejected and guilt needled me. "She's my best friend."

"Ashfords do not associate with that family."

He rolled his eyes, a big mistake. "Don't you think this is all a little stupid?" Another mistake.

Dad leaned forward, his brows drawing together. "Listen to me, you ignorant child, this is not up for discussion. Those people do not deserve to kiss the ground you walk upon." He threw the phone back at Carter. It smacked him in the chest. "Text her back. Tell her you'll be there soon."

"What?" Carter looked at me again, but I didn't know what Dad was playing at.

"Meet her where?" I asked.

Dad met my gaze. "Carter is going to tell us once and for all where their secret spot is. Her text asked him to meet her there. And we wouldn't want to disappoint her, would we?"

I didn't like the sound of that. "Dad—"

"Conner, you will meet her."

I jerked back, remembering my earlier confrontation with her. I wasn't exactly jonesing for a repeat. "I don't think—"

"It isn't for you to think. All I want is for you to have a conversation with her. Say whatever you need to, and remind that little girl to stay away from Carter."

"Dad," Carter pleaded. "Please. Leave her alone."

"Where are you meeting her?" Dad asked.

Carter didn't respond.

"Would you rather I inform her parents of your plans to spend time together?"

Carter's eyes widened, and I guessed Lena's parents didn't want her spending time with an Ashford either. "Fine." He closed his eyes. "There's a spot by the boardwalk." We already knew that much. "It's hidden among the rocks. The only road to get back there is a dirt path."

Wonderful, I'd have to get my car washed after this.

"Conner." Dad pointed to the door.

I got the hint and stood, unable to look at my brother as I walked out.

I was almost to my car when Carter came running up behind me. "Conner, stop."

With a sigh, I faced him. "You know I don't have a choice, right?"

"Yes." He pushed a hand through his unruly hair. "None of us ever have a choice. Just … Lena is a good person, okay. Better than any of us. I want to protect her."

I didn't like Lena Contreras. She was combative and pushy, but it wasn't like I couldn't see her appeal. She was also beautiful and feisty and strong. She didn't back down, and I had to respect that. My brother obviously did.

"It'll be okay, Carter. I won't be rough on her."

He seemed to relax at that. Whatever his relationship was with my father, Carter trusted me, I could see it in his eyes. And I wanted to earn that trust more than I wanted much of anything else.

I put a hand on his shoulder. "I tried to convince him not to change the trust. It wasn't my doing."

"I know." He backed up. "It's never your fault, but you do what he says anyway."

That hurt, but I couldn't blame him. He watched me get in my car and drive off toward the boardwalk at the edge of town. Dust kicked up beneath my tires as I turned onto the dirt road that led down to the water and the rocky jetty that extended out into the bay.

In the distance, I caught sight of the rocks, a last line of defense against the churning bay. As I neared, I slowed until the car came to a stop.

There she was.

Standing on a tall, uneven rock, Lena looked down into the water, showing no fear at the prospect of tumbling off. Dark hair fell forward as she leaned farther out over the water, concealing her face from view.

But I knew it was her. There had always been something so unique about Lena, the way she moved. I'd deny noticing if anyone asked, but I'd never been able to help it.

Even when she was yelling at me, which happened quite often.

At the sound of my car door slamming, she turned. I saw it in slow motion. Her foot slipped, and she lost her balance.

I sprinted forward, barely managing to catch her around the waist to prevent her from falling into the bay. She collapsed into me, sending us both sprawling to the ground.

Rolling off me immediately, she lay on her back, her breath wheezing. After a minute, a small laugh escaped her.

I pushed myself up, brushing grass from my pants. "What is so funny?"

As if seeing who I was for the first time, her smile dropped. "Oh, it's you."

I didn't like the sound of that. "You're welcome." I walked away from the rocks.

"For what?" She got to her feet. "Nearly startling me into the bay?"

"No, no, don't worry about it, Lena. It was nothing. You don't need to thank me."

She growled—yes, growled—and turned away from me, climbing over a rock to get down to a tiny strip of beach. So, that was where Carter brought the small fishing boat he didn't think I knew he used.

I followed her, getting down to the beach the same way she had.

"What do you want, Conner? Haven't we seen enough of each other today?"

"I have a proposition for you." I'd thought of this on the drive over. A way to get her to back away from Carter. Their friendship only caused problems.

She faced me, her arms crossed. "A proposition? This should be good."

I didn't appreciate her sarcasm but was also strangely drawn to it. I wanted her to keep talking. Clearing my throat and pushing those thoughts from my mind, I started, "You want to buy my family's land."

She lifted one brow. "And? I thought that was never going to happen, as you so graciously told me this morning."

Man, I'd been a jerk. "I'm sorry, okay."

"Sorry? You? Ha."

"Just listen to me." She wasn't making this easy. "I'll convince my father to sell."

Her face brightened, but there was also a wariness in her eyes. "There's a catch. Always is with your family. Just tell me what it is."

I sucked in a breath, knowing the next words out of my mouth were a betrayal of my brother. Was I really doing this? Yes, apparently. "You have to stay away from Carter."

All light faded from her eyes, all hope that what I'd offer was a good deal. It wasn't. This was terrible. I was about to make her choose between her business and her best friend. My father had tried to teach all his kids friendships were liabilities. It seemed three of his four children took it to heart.

Now, I was trying to force that reality on the only one of us who never had.

Lena's jaw tensed. "No." She turned and climbed down the rocks toward the strip of beach.

"No?" I scrambled after her. "It's what you want, the land. It's a good deal, Lena."

I'd almost reached her when she turned on her heel, anger flashing in those deep brown eyes. "A good deal? You want me to give up my oldest friend for a parcel of land? You're a real piece of work, Conner Ashford. Just like your father." She towered over me from her perch on the rocks.

I climbed up the rocky slope until we were eye level. "You know nothing about my father."

"But I know plenty about you."

I was so close I could feel her breath. "Oh, really? Enlighten me then. What do you think you know about me?"

Her eyes narrowed in challenge. "You're cold. The only thing that matters to you is business and your family's image. There's more to life than what other people think of us, Conner."

"Like I thought, you know nothing."

"And you know so much about me?" She lifted her chin. "This feud between our families is stupid, but even if it wasn't there, I'd never want to get to know someone like you. And you'd never know me. That would require you to see anyone other than yourself. Like your brother, for instance. What would he think of your little offer? An offer I reject, in case you hadn't surmised as much."

I couldn't take my eyes off hers, the way her pupils dilated as she grew more angry. Angry Lena was a force, and she had principals. A quality I never knew I admired so much. Her loyalty to my brother was something to see.

She heaved a breath. "You could never understand what it's like to have a friend who gets every part of you. That would require you to surrender this stony strength you seem to think is such an asset. You know, being a jerk will never be a good thing."

"Do you ever stop talking?" I couldn't halt the words before they spilled out.

Lena's lips clamped shut, and she stared at me for a long moment. At any second, I expected flames to come shooting out of her nose, to burn in her eyes. Which was probably how I hadn't seen it coming.

I was so focused on her intense gaze I didn't feel her hand on me until it was too late. She shoved me through a gap in the rocks, and unlike with her, there was no one willing to catch me before I tumbled off the edge.

Chapter Seven

CONNER

I tried to sneak in through the sliding glass door from the patio, not wanting my dad or my grandfather to see me return home dripping wet. Not like that was the worst outcome of Lena pushing me into the bay.

The leather seats of my Mercedes were now sopping with bay water. I'd have to get someone to clean it out.

Our housekeeper, Mrs. Cramer, stood in the kitchen when I entered, her eyes going wide. "What in the world happened to you?"

"Don't ask." I was going to get back at Lena. She'd pushed me in, and by the time I swam back to the small beach, she was gone, leaving me with a key fob that no longer worked, and a ruined phone.

She'd regret every action. I'd make sure of it.

I'd almost made it to the stairs that spiraled up to my wing of the house when someone cleared their throat. I closed my eyes for a brief moment before turning to find my grandfather watching. His brow arched toward his gray hair.

"You know, Conner, you're supposed to wear a bathing suit

if you're going to take a dip." He had the decency to bite back his laughter.

"I don't want to talk about it."

"Too late for that, I'd say." Glee danced in his eyes, and it reminded me of Carter. Granddad was so different from his son, it was hard to imagine him raising someone as cold as my father. He once ran the winery and the vineyard, but in tandem with his wife. They hadn't expanded it quite like my father had, being content running a smaller operation, though it still generated more profit than most.

My father liked to say Grandad's greatest flaw was a lack of ambition. I never saw it that way. He didn't yearn for power, for control. He had money, lots of it, but he never used it to exert his influence.

"Go on." I sighed. "I know you have some jokes in you."

Granddad grinned. "Thanks for your permission. Wouldn't want you to be a wet blanket."

"That was just bad."

"Oh, go cry me a river ... or a bay as apparently you've been doing."

"Oh, man." I rubbed my eyes. His jokes were getting worse with age.

"We have washing machines, you know. You didn't have to clean your clothes in the bay."

"I'm going upstairs now." I started climbing.

His voice trailed after me. "I know there are plenty of people who wish you'd swim with the fishies, but I don't think this is what they meant." Did my grandfather just say there were people who wanted me dead?

I shook my head as I changed into dry clothes. Well, at least he was good at taking the edge off my anger. I suspected he knew exactly what he was doing.

When I went back downstairs, I found both my father and grandfather in the library. I didn't spend much time in there as the room was tinged with the smell of tobacco from my father's pipe.

"Conner," his gruff voice called. "Come here."

I entered tentatively, waiting for my father to speak again.

"Well, what did the girl say?"

At the mere mention of Lena, anger curled in my gut. "She won't listen to a word that comes out of my mouth. That girl is infuriating."

"Hmm ..." My father crossed his legs where he sat in a high-backed leather chair.

Granddad pretended to read on the couch.

"We can't let her get the land." Not after she practically laughed in my face about the deal. I sat on the open end of the stiff couch.

"No, we won't sell to her." He seemed to be thinking hard. "But it won't be enough."

"Is that where you were, Conner?" Granddad asked. "Talking to the Contreras girl?" I could see his mind working, putting the pieces together, how I'd come home soaking wet. He suppressed a smile. "Interesting." He murmured something about the apple not falling far from the orchard.

A nose nudged my hand, and I curled my fingers into Duke's fur, letting some of the anger ebb away like it tended to do when he was around. It had been a long time since I had a good human friend, but he was ten times better than most humans.

Something my dad didn't understand when he scowled at the dog's presence.

Tearing his glare from Duke, Dad pinned his gaze on me. "We need to find out more about this plan of hers. If the Contreras family intends to expand their business, we will make sure it doesn't happen."

"You don't get it, Dad." Duke lay his head on my lap, looking up at me with wide chocolate eyes that seemed to be saying it wasn't okay to try to defeat her. What did he know? He was a dog. "Lena ... she's not like normal people. She won't make mistakes, she won't give up. Her plans ... no matter what we decide about the land, she will reach her goals. I've never seen anyone with so little quit in them. She won't back down." I'd never been more sure of anything.

"Sounds like you admire this girl." Granddad's voice was quiet, soft.

"No, I just ..." What? Did I admire her? Respect her? "I don't want us to deceive ourselves."

Dad stood. "I know that family, Conner. Sooner or later, she will sink herself." He walked out, issuing a sharp, "Dad, we have business to attend to."

Granddad stood more slowly. "I don't know what I did wrong with that man, but apparently he now needs me for business he's pushed me out of the last few years."

I knew the truth. Dad just wanted Granddad away from me for fear he'd encourage my admiration.

When they were gone, I leaned my head back, staring up at the ornate wooden bookcases.

I didn't even hear Carter come in.

"You're right, you know." A sigh hissed past his lips as he took Dad's vacated seat.

I didn't look at him. "That's not a phrase I hear much from you."

That earned me a chuckle. "Well, because you're usually a colossal jerk. But about Lena ... there isn't anything an Ashford can do to stop her once she sets her mind to something."

"Dad will try."

"And you?"

I was quiet for a long moment. "She pushed me into the bay."

A loud laugh barked out of him. "I'd have paid good money to see that."

"She refuses to end your friendship."

I could practically hear his smile, it was so wide. "Never any doubt."

I slid my eyes along the room until they met his. "Are you in love with her? Tell me you are because I don't understand what else could be worth all this trouble."

He didn't answer for a long moment. "No." That surprised me. "I'm not *in* love with her, but I do love her. I feel sorry for you, Conner, that you don't get it. Friendship … it's worth disappointing Dad for, it's worth having more restrictions put on my trust, it's worth more than any amount of money." He stood. "If you try to interfere again, you'll see just how much I'm willing to give up for her."

He walked out, leaving me with a giant pit in my stomach. How had today happened? I'd gone from fighting her in the downtown streets, to trying to persuade her to abandon my brother, to being pushed in the bay.

I couldn't be in this house any longer. I needed a distraction.

Through all the tasks of running the business, there was only one I cared about. Making wine.

"Come on, Duke." He whined after Carter, but as soon as I patted my leg, he followed me outside and across the lawn to the barn that held both my office and the small wine press.

In a meticulously clean room, a room that looked nothing like the inside of a barn, barrels of various wines were stacked along the far wall. I'd equipped the space with all the gear I needed to experiment with small batches, combining various kinds of grapes, as well as trying out some of the rarer hybrid grapes I cultivated myself in small quantities.

I loved the science behind wine making. It got me out of my own head, let me forget this awful day.

And almost wiped the image of beautiful brown eyes and dark hair from my mind.

Duke whined at me, as if he could sense the direction of my thoughts. "I'm trying to be better, buddy." I didn't want to end up like my father, revered but not exactly liked. Alone, save for children who were scared of him and a father who was disappointed in him.

Duke leaned against my leg as I filled a glass from one of the wines I just bottled last night. I took a sip, letting the sweet liquid flow down the back of my throat and hit every taste bud.

It was missing something.

Seemed like that was going around.

Chapter Eight

LENA

"*Mi cielito*, be careful with that step ladder." My mother, ever the worry wart, clucked at me like one of her chickens.

"I'm fine, *Mami*. I've been training apple trees since I was five."

"But that one time you fell off the ladder."

"I was eight." I rolled my eyes, tying a length of soft twine around the slim branch of a two-year tree. Training trees was mindless work, but it took the whole family and most of our skeletal staff to get the work done every year. We usually finished by mid-May, but this year, with fewer hands, it was taking us longer.

Enzo moved on to the rows of three-year trees with the taller ladder, barely hiding his amusement as he worked quietly with our dad.

Wiping the sweat from my brow, I climbed down the stepladder and moved to the next tree. Mom removed the training ties from last year, giving a nod of approval when last year's solid branches stayed put without the ties. Apple trees craved sunlight, and they produced the best fruit when the bulk of the trunk wood was exposed to it. I tied down the new growth to train future branches to remain wide open to the sky.

"It's going to be a good harvest this year, *Mija*. The fruit buds are looking lovely already."

"Music to my ears." I tied a branch down, securing it with a heavy rock so the tender young branch arched down toward the ground. As it continued to mature throughout the season, the branch would harden and remain in this ideal position permanently. A good harvest this year would make up for the last few harvests that hadn't fared as well. It would be a small step in the right direction, but we still had a long road ahead of us.

If my family would trust me. I knew I could breathe new life into Orchard Hill Farm, but I needed them to listen to me and not hear little Lena with the big dreams. That was hard when your family still saw you as the kid in pigtails, skinning her knees from climbing trees with the boys.

"What's on your mind, Lena?" Grams asked, handing me a cool glass of lemonade from the truck.

"The usual." I sighed, moving into the shade for a rest. "Work. Things that need to be done around here. More work."

"And secret bank loans for secret Selena projects?" my grandmother whispered in a hushed voice.

"Grams." I shushed her, looking over my shoulder to see if Mom heard us. She would not approve. Neither would Dad.

"I'm not sharing your secrets, Lena. I have faith in you. But the Ashfords can be a sly bunch. As soon as you attempt to make big moves for Orchard Hill, they will swoop in like vultures to push you back down."

"So, I shouldn't try?"

Grams gave me a dirty look for putting words in her mouth.

"Of course you should *try*. You just have to be smart about it. Smarter than all of them put together. You will find a way to get the loans you need."

"How can I when the Ashfords refuse to sell the land I need? As soon as they found out a Contreras was the interested buyer, they rejected my offer." I turned back to my work, gathering a bundle of training ties for the saplings we planted last week.

"If I know the Ashfords at all, they'll want something other than money."

"If it was just money, I would find a way."

"They want something that will hurt?"

I nodded. "They want me to stop seeing Carter." I looked up at the clear afternoon sky, wishing I was anywhere but here. The mindless activity left me free to think about all the things. Plans for Orchard Hill led to thoughts of how to make it happen and thoughts of buying the property I needed. Then, Carter's betrayal and Conner Ashford, which sent me into a fury.

Though the last time I'd seen him was a supremely satisfying moment, I would likely regret it. Dumping the heir to Ashford Estates into the bay was not the best way to get ahead in this town.

"I've been telling you for years, your friendship with that boy will come to no good. Trust me, I know."

"I trust him." Grams and I walked along the fresh mounds of new saplings. This would require a more delicate hand to train the youngest saplings. Grams was the best at this particular chore.

She sat down on the ground, talking to the baby trees in Spanish. She claimed they responded more to the romance of the Spanish language. I wasn't so sure she was wrong.

"Of course you do, he is your friend. You two have been sneaking around since you were young. No friendship would last that long through such trials if it wasn't a true friendship. I didn't say I don't approve of the relationship."

It felt good that she understood, but I knew there was a 'but' coming.

"But his family will use him against you to get what they want. Ending your friendship with Carter would be the first of many conditions they would put on you. You don't want the Ashfords holding anything over your head, so don't give them a precedent."

"I won't let them manipulate me." I trimmed a spindly growth from the first sapling. "I'll find another way to get the land I need. I wanted the parcel close to town to draw in tourists and still remain close to Orchard Hill, but maybe we can make it work with something farther from town."

"Don't compromise on your dreams, *Mija*. You will find a way to get what you want. Just be careful. Old man Ashford is like your Carter, but his son and grandson are cut from a different cloth."

"Deep down, Conner is just a spineless coward."

"You work too hard." Grams shifted the loose soil around the root ball of the sapling. "You and your brother. You're too young to spend all your time working to keep this orchard afloat."

"We do what we have to, Grams." I smiled at my grand-mother. "There's nowhere else I'd rather be."

"Well, the old ones can handle the rest of this work." Grams climbed back to her feet. "Enzo, take your sister sailing." She dusted the dirt from her grandma jeans.

"You're not old, Grams." I leaned against her. I could try to talk her out of sending us sailing, but I knew from experience I would lose that argument. Plus, it had been an age since we went on the boat Enzo had fixed up two summers ago.

"Of course not, I'm talking about those two." She flung a

hand out at her son and daughter-in-law shuffling along the rows of young saplings.

"Right." I grinned at my grams, draping an arm around her. "Maybe you should come sailing with us and leave the olds to the work."

"But then, who will tell them what to do?" Grams dead-panned. I loved this woman. Of all my family, I felt the most connected with her. My mom was Mom. She was the best mother I could have asked for, but Grams was special.

"Sailing? Really?" Enzo glanced back over his shoulder at the others hard at work.

"Grams says I'm too young to work so hard, so you have to take me out for a leisurely afternoon on the bay."

Enzo tossed down his gloves, and with a shrug, he followed Grams' orders. "Won't argue with that." He grinned. "She's right, you need to get work off your mind for a while, and I have a new fishing rod to break in."

Chapter Nine

CONNER

I cracked open my second beer for the day. I wasn't normally a beer drinker, but there was something about spending an afternoon on the boat with my brothers in the open waters of the bay that just demanded an ice cold beer.

"You've got some catching up to do, Conner." Carter climbed up the steps onto the terrace, dripping seawater onto the deck.

"You know I don't do the public intoxication thing. Besides, someone has to be sober enough to drive us back home, and it can't be Duke." I ran my fingers through Duke's wiry, brindled fur. He was a good sailor, just not the best swimmer, so he was sporting his red life preserver today.

"First, it isn't public if the only people here are your brothers and Harrison." Carter patted himself down with a fluffy beach towel, careful not to spill his beer. Harrison lobbed a bottle cap at him for the slight. He might be our cousin, but he was pretty much one of the brothers.

"Second, that's not what I meant. When was the last time you and that mangy mutt of yours spent an afternoon at the pool or out on the boat?" He shielded his eyes like the glare from my skin blinded him.

"Duke, he called you a mutt!" I pulled my dog close to my side. "Duke would have you all know he comes from a long line of prize-winning Irish Wolfhounds."

"You are sporting a pretty impressive farmer's tan." Conrad ignored me and my dog as he glanced over from his lounge chair. His own perfect tan said he spent a lot of time outdoors without a shirt on, but Conrad was a hard worker. He broke from tradition and left the family business to become a large animal veterinarian and the savior of the Corolla Wild Horse Sanctuary in Superiore Bay.

I ignored both of them and continued sipping my beer, enjoying the rare afternoon away from work. Duke was enjoying himself too. He lay stretched out to his full length in the sun, tongue lolling out as I reached to scratch his belly. Ashford Vineyards was my life, and most of the time I enjoyed the work, but it tended to leave little else for me.

"Seriously, buddy, you need to get away from those grapes more often," Harrison said, his tone drowsy from under his hat. He lay sprawled out on the sofa beside me.

"So says the hardware store owner-slash-firefighter-slash-mayor." Harrison was just as busy as I was, but he still knew when to leave work at work.

"Volunteer firefighter," Harrison mumbled. "It's not a full-time commitment."

"But running this town is probably an eighty-hour-a-week job." I drained the last of my drink before it had time to grow warm. Warm beer was the worst.

"Depends on the week." Harrison rolled over onto his back and immediately fell asleep, making me think he was midway through a very long week.

Sweat beaded my forehead. The cold drink had chased away the heat of the day for a brief moment, but a dip in the bay would fix that for good. "I'm going for a swim," I announced to my dozing brothers. They were all several drinks ahead of me and enjoying their sunbathing. Duke was sound asleep.

The bay was calm today, and the breeze rushed warm across my skin as I stood at the edge of the beach terrace on the family yacht—one of several. It was one of those rare, truly hot summer days Maine seldom saw, and I was glad I'd let Carter bully me into ditching work to join them. But that water was going to be cold. No matter what time of year it was, the bay waters were always cold.

I knew better than to turn my back to my brothers. Even asleep, they couldn't be trusted. The swift kick to my butt sent me flying through the air to belly flop into the ocean. The sting of the cold water numbed my skin as I floundered for the surface.

"Carter!" I spewed salt water from my mouth. Duke echoed my accusation with a bark and a growl of solidarity.

"How do you know it was me? It could have been Conrad." Carter didn't even have the decency to help me back up the steps.

"That's it, pick on Conner day is over." I slicked my hair back and lunged for Carter, pulling him up and tossing him into the bay, fresh beer and all.

Conrad chuckled from his comfortable spot on the lounge, and Harrison snored, but I wasn't done. I grabbed Conrad's hand and pulled him to his feet.

"Don't do it, Conner." Conrad pushed back.

"Oh, it's happening." I shouldered him toward the edge of the boat. He was built like a brick wall, but we grappled, laughing like we had when we were kids. Still, I was the second oldest but also the tallest, and I always won these fights. Conrad went in headfirst, and I turned for Harrison, who was still asleep and unsuspecting.

Gripping the edge of the sofa, I slid him across the deck and dumped him into the ocean before he knew what was happening. He came up sputtering. "What did I miss?"

"Come on, Duke!" With a triumphant grin, I dove into the bay to join my brothers. They were right, I needed to relax more often. Working with our father had made me too serious.

Duke barked from the yacht, growling at us like we'd all lost our minds. He was a crap swimmer, but he was wearing his giant doggy life vest. "Come on, boy!" Carter whistled, and Duke whined as he lowered his front end, his big doggy butt sticking up in the air.

"You can do it, buddy, just come down the steps." I swam toward the deck so he knew I would catch him if he sank. With a yelp like a puppy, he jumped, long legs flailing as he hit the water.

"Good boy." I reached for him as he paddled toward me, draping a reassuring arm around his middle.

"Good boy, Duke!" Harrison clapped, and Duke showed his toothy grin, paddling for all he was worth. Once he realized he wasn't going to sink with his life jacket on, he relaxed and bobbed up and down in the gentle waves like a cork.

The swim in the crisp cold water was invigorating, but even at play, my mind drifted back to work and the ten thousand things I had waiting for me on my desk when I returned. Specifically, I had a potential new contract with a small buyer in New Hampshire to review. The family owned several B&Bs in the area and were interested in stocking one of my private label hybrid wines as part of their special monthly wine tasting events at each of their locations. It wasn't a landmark deal that would get my father's attention, but it was a big deal for me. Working with my hybrid wines was the only thing that kept me going most days.

"Look at him, he's thinking about those fancy grapes again."

Carter splashed my face. "You can tell because his eyes get all dreamy like he's thinking about a girl."

"Shut up." I splashed him back and headed for the deck. "It's time to head back in, guys. I've got work."

"We all have work, Conner." Conrad lunged toward me, and I was underwater, arms flailing before I came up sputtering for the second time today.

"Except maybe Carter," Harrison quipped.

"Hey, I have work, of a sort." My younger brother grinned.

"Come on, guys, help me get this giant dog back up on the boat." I guided Duke to the lounge terrace steps that lowered right into the water. I pulled myself up onto the first step and coaxed Duke to place his front paws on the step beside me. "Give his rear a push, Carter."

Duke whimpered. He didn't like steps. Really, it wasn't so much that he disliked them as it was he didn't understand them. Or his size. He was easily a hundred and forty pounds, but he thought he was a third of that.

"Jeez, Conner, what are you feeding him?" Carter shouldered Duke up the steps until the gentle giant figured out how to lumber up to the terrace deck.

"He's still carrying a little holiday weight, so don't make him feel bad." I sat on the steps and gave each of my brothers a hand up into the boat.

"Are you still making his food yourself?" Conrad asked, eyeing the dog with a veterinarian's eye.

"Yeah, and he eats about a metric ton every month. Takes me a whole week to make enough to last him six weeks."

"Best thing you could do for him." Conrad clapped him on the shoulder. "Oh, watch out, Carter, he's going to shake."

The three of us ducked as Duke stood at the center of the terrace, shaking the seawater from his coat. "Sorry, dude, you're going to smell like wet dog for the rest of the day." I grinned at Carter as I came up the steps to the deck.

Carter just muttered something about crazy dogs and their stupid dads as he tossed me a fresh towel.

"Come on, Duke, get in your bed." I pointed to the plush dog bed beside the couch. "Get your teddy." Duke grabbed his tattered teddy bear from the lounge and folded his long frame on the bed, resting his chin on his favorite toy we couldn't go anywhere without.

"Uh, bad news, guys." Harrison jogged down the steps from the flybridge. "We're stuck. It won't start."

"What do you mean it won't start?" I asked.

"Exactly what it sounds like. The engine won't start. We're going to need a tow."

"That could take hours." Conrad groaned. "I have to get back to the sanctuary before Amelia leaves on the last ferry."

"Let me try it." I headed up the stairs to the main deck, all three brothers behind me. There was no way the engine wasn't working. The yacht couldn't be more than a few years old, and Dad was meticulous about keeping the family fleet in top condition.

We crowded into the upper flybridge, and I immediately saw the problem. "You didn't lift the anchor first." I pulled the lever to retract the anchor and waited until I could feel us drifting with the current. "Now, you start the engine." I flipped the switch and waited for the hum of power beneath my feet. Nothing happened.

"Told you." Conrad shrugged.

"So, we're stuck, and now we're drifting." Carter stared at all the dials and switches on the helm.

I tried the engine again and again.

"Watch out. You'll flood it," Harrison said.

"What does that even mean?" Carter asked.

I tried it again. I didn't know what it meant either.

"I don't know, but it's what you say when someone tries the

engine too frequently." Harrison swatted my hand away from the ignition switch.

"Conrad, don't you know how to fix tractors and stuff on the farm?" I turned to my brother, hoping he could save the day.

"It's a horse sanctuary, not a farm, and I don't own a tractor. If something breaks down, I call a mechanic."

"We're never going to get a tow in the middle of the after-noon on a weekday." Carter shook his head. "The coastguard is way out at sea by now, and no one's on the bay today."

"We could send up a flare?" Harrison suggested.

"No way. We'll never hear the end of it." I grabbed my phone from where I'd left it at the helm and moved out to the open bow deck, checking for a signal. "The *Weekly Wine* would be all over this. Local rich boys send up rescue flare when their million dollar yacht won't start. That's not happening."

"Did it cost that much?" Carter eyed the luxury around us.

"I don't know." I shrugged, trying to make a call despite the lack of service. We were far out from the mainland without another boat in sight.

Carter had the binoculars out, searching for anyone nearby, and I went to try the engine again.

"You're going to flood it," Harrison reminded me.

"We don't even know what that means," I snapped at him, feeling useless. Between the four of us, one of us should have the skills to fix this situation. I was feeling my privilege like never before. I should know how to deal with this, but I didn't have a clue.

"Hey, I see a boat!" Carter ducked into the cabin and laid on the horn while the other two waved them down.

Maybe this wouldn't be so bad. The boat was big enough to give us a tow to the yacht club at the north end of the bay.

I went out to join my brothers, waving at the approaching

fishing boat. If this didn't take too long, I could be back at my desk, elbows deep in vendor contracts before the afternoon was a complete waste.

I lifted my hand, ready to shout my thanks when a familiar brown-haired figure waved back. "Oh, crap."

Chapter Ten
LENA

"Oh, crap." I groaned, dropping my hand to shield my eyes. Freaking Conner Ashford, of all people.

"We're in it now, Lena." Enzo steered our ancient fishing boat alongside the smallest of the Ashford family's yachts. "Not like we can leave them stranded."

"You sure about that?" I avoided Carter's face-splitting grin. I was still mad at him. Tried to be anyway, but I could never stay mad at him for long.

"Enzo!" Carter whistled. "Mr. Fix-it himself."

"What's the problem?" Enzo dropped the anchor, and we bobbed in the calm waters beside the luxury forty-foot yacht that probably cost more than Orchard Hill Farms was worth.

"Won't start." Harrison Ashford shrugged. "And we're useless."

"Speak for yourself." Conner punched his cousin in the shoulder.

"Wait here." Enzo left the helm and boarded the yacht.

"Not likely." I followed him. If he needed any help, those four weren't it.

I tumbled onto the deck, slamming my hip, and was greeted

by a massive brindled dog wearing a red doggy life jacket around his middle. He towered over me, sniffing my hair, and I wasn't sure I should move. He had eyes like a wolf, but he wasn't growling.

"Duke, give the lady some room." Conner absently called his dog back, but Duke had other plans. I scrambled back to my feet, and the giant dog sat back on his haunches, nudging my hand for head scratches. I didn't even have to bend over to pet him. His head came up to my waist. "Well, you're just a big sweetie, aren't you?" I murmured, scratching behind his ears. "Too bad your dad's a big land-grabbing meanie." Duke and I went to join the others standing around speculating about what could be the trouble.

"Did you guys check the engine?" I asked, turning to Carter. I might be mad at him, but he was the only Ashford brother I'd willingly speak to.

"Uh." Carter scratched his head. "I'm not even sure I know where it is."

Enzo chuckled and made his way down from the flybridge to the lower deck. All the Ashfords followed like little ducklings. I rolled my eyes and elbowed my way through the rich boys to help my brother open the fancy hatch in the floor.

"Does she sound flooded?" Enzo asked, and I snickered at their blank stares.

"Probably after Conner tried starting it a million times," Carter offered.

"Did not." Conner swatted at his brother. "And don't act like you even know what that means. Duke, seriously, leave her alone." He snapped his fingers to get the dog's attention. But Duke was my new bestie. I gave him shoulder scratches, and he leaned into me, eating up the attention.

Enzo climbed down the ladder into the small space below deck. As far as engine rooms went, this was the cleanest one I'd ever seen.

"What's that noise?" Conrad leaned down into the hatch.

"Sounds like you're overheated," I supplied. "You should have seen an alarm flash on the helm." I watched as Enzo checked the engine water intake system. Sure enough, he pulled out a plastic bag and some other debris.

"How'd that get in there?" Carter asked.

"People throw their garbage into the bay, and it's bound to get sucked into your engines." Enzo looked up at the brothers. "Lena, go give it a try, I'm not sure that's the only problem."

I waved Carter off and trotted back up to the flybridge, Duke leading the way like a gentleman escort, passing through the main salon and galley. These Ashfords really knew how to do luxury.

Duke let out a terrifying bark and sat back on his haunches, looking at me like he knew I could figure this out. Smart dog. "Ugh, really?" I flipped off the silent alarm flashing red on the dash. "They never even noticed that, did they?" Duke gave a massive yawn.

I tried the ignition. Nothing. They were either out of fuel or they had air or water in the fuel system.

Duke and I headed back to the boys, shoving through the Ashfords to get to Enzo. "Nothing." I shook my head. "How's their fuel?"

"Nearly a full tank," Enzo answered.

"Air?" I asked, and he nodded, turning to climb up the ladder.

"What's that mean?" Carter asked.

"Lena's right, you probably have air in the fuel system. We'll give you a tow to the marina on the south side."

"Air in the fuel system? That sounds bad." Conner scratched his chin. "We should take it to the Bay Club on the north side."

Enzo shook his head. "It's an easy fix. You probably have a leak in the pipe between the fuel tank and the injection pump.

But we're closer to south side, and we don't have the horse-power to haul you all the way into the Bay Club."

"Fine. We'll call for another tow once we're in." Conner dismissed us like we were servants and not good Samaritans helping them out of the goodness of our hearts.

"The south side marina could fix it easy," Enzo suggested. "It's not a big repair, and they could use the business."

"My father would prefer to have the Bay Club specialists look at it. It's a rather expensive boat, you know."

"Sure, sure." Enzo nodded. "Let's get you boys rigged and back to shore. Lena, can you pull ahead, and I'll toss you the towlines."

Carter started clapping and hooting like a buffoon. "Lena, you're my hero!" He draped an arm around me, whispering, "Don't be mad," in my ear.

"Oh, wipe the grin off your face." I shoved past him, clambering from the fancy deck, over the rail and back on our perfectly fine fishing boat that had seemed a bit luxurious to me before I set foot on the Ashford yacht. The name of the boat caught my eye as I maneuvered around to the bow. *Dad's Handmedown.* I'd bet just about anything the old man re-named the boat before he handed it over to his kids to play with. *What a life.*

Duke barked at me from the bow deck on the yacht, and I called back to him. He was a great dog. If he was smaller, I'd put him in my bag and take him home with me.

I caught the towlines from Enzo and secured them, leaving a healthy distance between the two boats. I watched my brother waving his hands and talking loudly to make sure the Ashford's knew how this was going to go. Slow and steady. Enzo was right, we didn't have the horsepower to tow them very far, so we were going to have to let the current help us.

"You think they have a clue what they're doing with that big boat?" I called over my shoulder as I turned toward the south side marina, the tug of the huge yacht behind us like an anchor pulling us back.

"That's a hard, fast no." Carter came to stand beside me, and I did a double take, looking for my brother.

"Enzo thought it best if he stayed back there in case my brothers do something stupid or anyone needs to make a quick, smart decision."

I snorted a laugh, trying to keep my 'I'm mad at you' scowl in place.

"Come on, Lena." He laid a hand on my shoulder. "I'm sorry I let Conner ambush you. I would have warned you, but my dad saw your text, and he took my phone."

"What are you, twelve?" Really, the way the old man treated his adult children was kind of embarrassing. I couldn't imagine sticking around with my hand out, letting him treat me like that just because he controlled the money. In Carter's shoes, I'd just make my own way and let the old man bully the others. But I didn't know what it felt like to be in Carter's shoes, so that was probably easier said than done.

"It's complicated. Dad's a tyrant, but he's not going to tell me who I can be friends with. I'm just sorry about Conner. He was a little wet when he came home from our spot." His mouth twitched with amusement.

"He went for an unscheduled swim." I pushed our speed up a tiny bit, inching us along at a painfully slow rate. "Is he always such a jerk?"

"Who, Conner? No. Sometimes. He's just not so good at the social, talking to people thing. Don't let his stuffy businessman facade fool you, he's just trying to live up to all the pressure of being the next in line to run the family empire."

I did not want to feel sorry for Conner Ashford. "I guess your dad probably isn't the easiest to work with."

"Conner's pretty good at dealing with Dad. He's been going head to head with him since we were all kids. Conner always put himself between us and Dad, taking the brunt of his crap for us. The pressure I'm talking about comes from the town. He's got big shoes to fill. I'm just glad I was born third."

"Seriously, stop. I don't want to feel bad for him." I shoved Carter's face away with a laugh. I really couldn't stay mad at him for long.

"I'm not going to let my family bully you. I know you want that land, Lena. I don't know if I can help you get it. Dad got his hackles up the moment he realized a Contreras was interested in it."

"I'll figure something out."

"I was thinking I could help you look for other options. There has to be a piece of land around here somewhere that would work for your plans that my family doesn't own."

"You would think." It was sweet of him to offer the help, but there was a reason I wanted that parcel. It was close to town on the north side, without being too far from Orchard Hill Farm. It was perfect for tourism, and I wanted it. "I'm not done fighting yet, Carter." I gunned the engine, heading closer to land.

It was time to dump the Ashfords at the marina—get an eye full of them rubbing elbows with the fishermen at the Rusty Hook bait and tackle shop/boat mechanic—and get back to plotting.

Chapter Eleven

CONNER

Lena Contreras had never made sense to me. We weren't exactly new to each other. Our families operated on opposite edges of this town for so long I couldn't remember a time we didn't know each other.

But I'd never really known her. I scrubbed a hand across my face as I sat on the upper deck of the *Handmedown*. From here, I could see the entire marina in all its rugged glory. There was a reason I hadn't wanted to come here.

Fisherman wandered the worn and cracked wooden planks of the docks, coming in with their day's catch. Next to us, a mechanic yelled orders to someone from the engine room—if it could be called that—of a small pleasure boat, one that looked like it had seen better days.

This was a side of Superiore Bay I rarely saw. If we were at the Bay Club, a specialist would have already come to us, prioritizing our time over anyone else's. We'd have been brought drinks and anything else we wanted from the restaurant.

My eyes drifted to the Rusty Hook tackle shop at the center of all the activity. A small lobster shack stood beside it where people could walk up to a window and get all sorts of fried and greasy offerings. It turned my stomach just thinking about dockside food.

This part of town had seen better days, yet it thrummed with life.

Carter dropped into a chair next to me. "Enzo talked to a mechanic. We're in the queue."

"In the queue?"

"Yeah, like a line." He eyed me. "It's what normal people wait in."

I tried not to let my exasperation show, but I really needed to get back to work. And there was no way I was leaving the boat here with my brothers. Father would never forgive me if I put Carter in charge. Conrad knew less about boats than me, and our cousin Harrison was off talking with a crowd of fisherman who'd greeted him by name.

He wasn't the only one.

Lena walked along the dock, stopping to talk to everyone she saw, gracing them with the kind of smiles I'd never see from her. She stepped up beside Harrison, and the two of them started laughing about something. I found myself wishing I knew what had made her laugh.

Harrison was an Ashford. Carter was an Ashford. Yet, with me, that was suddenly a dirty word.

"It's because you treat her like she doesn't matter," Carter said as if he'd read my mind.

"What?"

"That look … you're confused about Lena because she's never this nice around you. I've been telling you for years she's great. She's just easy to rile up."

"Don't I know it." I didn't want to fight with her. I'd have even sold her the land if it were up to me, but it wasn't, and she saw that as my fault. "Something about her always makes me say things I don't mean."

Carter laughed. "Yeah, she has that effect on people."

"I wish we hadn't needed their help."

Carter stared at me for a long moment. "Conner ... what they did for us was nice, like really nice. We derailed their afternoon. Did you see the cooler of food and drinks and the brand-new fishing gear? I don't think they were planning to come back in before dinner."

I leaned forward, resting my elbows on my knees. "But why? What's in it for them?"

"Are you really so jaded you don't think people help others without getting anything in return?"

"Yes. That doesn't happen." Carter didn't understand. I couldn't accept charity from Lena and her brother. None of us should. I didn't want to owe anything to anyone.

Enzo walked toward us with an older man at his side. The man pushed sunglasses into his salt and pepper hair as he stared up at us. "You Ashford?"

I stood and climbed down the steps to the lower deck. "Sure am."

"This is Scooter." Enzo gestured to the man. "I explained what was going on to him."

Scooter nodded. "Air in the gas lines, eh? We can fix you up, no problem. I'll do a check for anything else that needs serviced. Give me a day or so." He handed me a clipboard. "Fill this out."

I scribbled my information down, not liking the informality of it, but at this point, I didn't have another choice.

Scooter took the clipboard and the keys then walked away without another word.

"You guys need a ride?" Enzo asked. "I have my truck in the lot. The bed is empty."

Riding home in the bed of a truck held no appeal. "No, we'll call for a car at the estate."

Enzo shrugged before turning and heading toward Lena.

They spoke and then walked toward the lot. She didn't even turn to say goodbye.

Carter ran after them and pulled her into a hug from behind. I couldn't take my eyes away from the ease of their relationship as she turned and swatted him with a laugh.

Bet she'd never push him into the bay.

I turned away from them and called Ashford Estates to have a car come take us to the Bay Club where we'd parked before heading out on the yacht. By the time we made it back to the house, the sun had set. Conrad and Harrison went their own ways, so only Carter walked inside with me. I'd completely given up on getting any more work done and just wanted a shower and my bed.

But when did I ever get what I wanted?

Carter slipped into the kitchen where I knew the cook would have left some dinner for us in the fridge. I walked by the library, planning to pick up my laptop and get out, but my grandfather sat among the books, an unlit pipe in hand.

"Going to smoke that?" I asked.

Grandfather looked at the pipe as if he was surprised it was there. "Oh, no. Just smelling it for now and thinking."

Getting my grandfather alone without my father was a feat. When I was younger, I'd taken to sneaking down here late at night when I knew he was still up. It was something I'd stopped as the years went on.

"Have a seat, Conner." He pointed to my father's favorite chair.

"I was actually going to go to bed." Even though it was too early for that, I was exhausted.

Grandfather only raised one eyebrow and waited.

Unable to deny him, I stayed. I didn't take my father's chair, instead opting for the couch.

"You look tired, Conner."

"I am. It's been a long day."

"I don't mean physically tired."

I sighed. "Am I ... capable?"

"What do you mean? You're the brightest young man I know."

I thought back to the boat, how I'd had no idea how to figure out what the problem was. I'd never felt more inept, and that didn't sit right with me. I excelled at things, I didn't bumble. "Yes, but life skills ..." I knew what I wanted to ask, but it was hard. "Would I be able to make it in the world without the Ashford name and fortune?"

"Ah, the age old question." He set his pipe on the table next to his chair. "The truth is, Conner, I don't know."

I started to respond, but he cut me off. "We only overcome the challenges we face, nothing more and nothing less. You can't fault yourself for not facing challenges that aren't yours, but at the same time, you need to be mindful of the incredible challenges others face who aren't as lucky as you."

I rested my elbow on the arm of the couch and leaned my head on my hand, my fingers sliding into my salt-crusted hair. "What about when we're the cause of challenges in someone else's life?" I couldn't get it out of my head.

He smiled. "The Contreras girl?"

I nodded. "Father is trying so hard to prevent her from getting her hands on our land, land we have no use for."

"Your father ..." He leaned his head back. "Did you know the Ashfords and the Contrerases used to be close?"

"I heard something like that, but it's hard to believe."

"It was before my time, but my mother used to tell me about those days when our two families were unstoppable. We would not be where we are if it was not for that partnership."

"But what about them? They struggle every year."

He gave me a sad look. "My father and grandfather took certain measures to hold them back."

"Just like my father is doing."

Grandfather looked at me for a long moment. "Your father took the rivalry to heart, something neither of his brothers did. But then, neither of his brothers stayed in the wine business either." My uncles got out of the family business with the blessing of my grandfather and then stayed near town, a part of our lives but also not.

My father hadn't reacted quite so kindly to Conrad leaving winemaking or Carter and Jorgina showing no interest in it as of yet.

"I don't know what to do." I rubbed my hand along the leg of my trunks. "Father wants me to do whatever is necessary to make sure Lena and her family never manage this business idea of theirs."

"I can't tell you what to do, Conner, but think of it like this: the worst thing that could happen is Lena succeeds, that she brings needed jobs and tourist dollars to Superiore Bay. Would that be so bad?"

"No." But to my father …

"You should never hope for someone to fail. That is when you become the kind of person I don't think you want to be."

Our conversation didn't last much longer and, after I showered, I crawled into bed. It should have been work on my mind, instead it was Carter's words to me.

Are you really so jaded you don't think people help others without getting anything in return?

I wished I could say he was wrong, that my grandfather's faith in me was well placed.

If I wanted to make anything right about this day, I knew what I needed to do, even if it meant swallowing my pride.

Chapter Twelve

LENA

"Stupid piece of garbage." I threw my wrench on the ground, wiping the sweat from my face with an old bandana I kept in my back pocket. It was really hot for May.

I kicked the tractor tire in frustration. I never should have let Enzo talk me into buying such an old pruning tower at that auction back in December. The thing hadn't worked right since we got it. But we needed the hydraulic lift this year. Our tallest standard apple trees were in desperate need of pruning. Most of our oldest fruit-bearing trees were over thirty feet tall, and if we wanted them to keep bearing good fruit, we needed to take care of them. Our best apples came from the part of the orchard where the trees were several generations old.

I bent over the pruning tower that would be hitched to our best tractor. Enzo and Dad were waiting for me, and daylight was fading. We had more than a dozen trees to prune before sunset if we were going to make it through the task this week.

A car door slammed, and a dog barked. Just what I needed. An unwanted distraction.

I turned toward the house, seeing a cloud of dust lingering

down the drive. The monster dog came darting around back, all legs and toothy smiles as he ran straight toward me.

"Woah, Duke." I held out my hands, hoping he wouldn't tackle me. "Nice to see you, boy." I got my hands into his fur as he skidded to a halt beside the pruning tower, dropping his butt on the ground and sniffing my pockets for treats. "Do you like apples, buddy? I got plenty of those." I scratched behind his ears. "I don't suppose you came alone?"

"He loves apples. Especially when they're covered in peanut butter." Conner Ashford came strolling into the backyard from the front drive. Dressed in khaki shorts, a snug fitting denim shirt, and flip flops, he looked like a walking ad for a men's magazine. Even his sunglasses were fancy—and probably cost more than my entire wardrobe. Certainly more than the piece of junk I was trying to salvage.

Around Orchard Hill, I was never too far from a barrel of apples. We had some Red Delicious apples waiting for a pickup beside the barn we used as a garage for old farm equipment. It was more like a graveyard these days. "Come on, Duke, let's get you a treat." I headed for the barn now, trying not to wonder what brought an Ashford to my house. It couldn't be anything good.

I sliced off a piece of apple with a pruning knife, and Duke gobbled it up.

"You can toss it on the ground, and he'll eat the whole thing in a few seconds. Just don't let him have the seeds." Conner stood in the dusty drive, hands shoved in his pockets with his designer messenger bag strapped over his shoulder.

I chatted with Duke, preferring his company as I cored the apple and let the big dog have at it. He was in heaven, chomping on the crunchy fruit like it was the meatiest bone. "Good boy." I patted his massive shoulder, walking with Conner back to the tractor.

"He likes you." Conner frowned at his dog like that was the strangest thing.

"And that's bad why?" I rolled my eyes and went back to work on the pruning tower. If the hydraulics could just hold my weight, it would be enough to get us through the pruning season. Maybe next year we could afford a mechanic. I bent to tighten another bolt.

"No, no, of course it's not." Conner backtracked, his tone sounding annoyed. "It's just … Duke likes people, but it takes him a while to warm up to strangers."

Duke nudged my hand, looking for more apples. Clearly, he did not view me as a stranger. But if I didn't know any better, I'd think Conner Ashford was flustered and a wee bit jealous of his dog.

I smiled at Duke. "Well." I looked up at Conner. "It seems that settles it."

"Settles what?"

I went back to work on the irritating bolt that refused to tighten. "Your dog has better taste than you do."

Conner laughed. "That's probably true."

I set the wrench back in my toolbox. That was as fixed as this thing was going to get. "Was there something you needed?" I shielded my eyes, looking up at Conner in all his windswept, casual glory. The man looked like he didn't know what a hard day's work was like.

"Oh, yes." He rummaged in his messenger bag. "I came to give you this. I appreciate your help the other day. We'd have been stuck out on the bay all night without your assistance." He handed me an envelope. I could tell by the way the sun shone through the thin paper there was a check in there with too many zeros. Zeros that would help us in more ways than Conner Ashford could imagine. But I wouldn't take his charity.

"Nonsense." I waved away the envelope. "We'd have helped anyone stranded out there."

"I insist." Conner pressed the check into my hand and stepped back. "It's the least I can do to repay you for the service you and your brother provided."

"For a kindness?" Was he for real? "Conner, it's called being a decent human being. Not a service. You call for a tow from the local marina, they come get you, you pay them. When a ... a neighbor happens upon you when you're having trouble, they lend a hand. No one expects payment for that." The Ashfords were a proud bunch, but even Conner couldn't be that clueless.

"I would feel better if you'd take it." He gestured at the barely functioning pruning tower. "Use it to fix this dinosaur. Let it be my way of helping Orchard Hill through a rough patch."

I snorted at that, shoving the envelope back into his hand. "You want to help us out, then sell me the land." I moved to hitch the tower to the tractor. I needed to get moving, and Conner was wasting my time. "Otherwise, we will earn the money that comes our way."

"Unfortunately, that's out of my hands."

"Aren't you the heir apparent? I thought the Ashfords made things happen in this town?" I climbed up into the tractor seat and found myself grinning back at him. He was too easy to needle.

"That doesn't make me a king, you know." Conner's mouth quirked into a smile. "Family is ... complicated sometimes." He gazed across the yard to the back porch where my grandmother and mother were trying to look like they weren't interested in what was happening.

"Speaking as one heir apparent to another." Conner shook his head. "I'm sorry for ambushing you the other day when you were waiting for Carter."

I shrugged. "Sorry for pushing you into the bay."

He laughed at that. "No, you aren't."

"You're right, that was actually the highlight of a very bad week, so thanks for that."

"I'd say anytime, but it was a miserable ride home."

"Good. Then, we're even." I nodded at the check he still held in his hand. "We helped you and your family. Payback for dumping you into the ocean in your expensive nice clothes."

"Fine," Conner relented. "We're even." He stuffed the check back into his bag, trying to hide his smile. It was the first time I'd seen a genuine smile or laugh from my best friend's big brother. I caught myself staring at the way the light played through his short, cropped hair. The russet auburn really shimmered in the sun.

"So, why won't you sell me the land, Ashford?" I knew I was pressing my luck, but when he wandered into my yard, he was going to answer my questions.

"You know our families don't see eye to eye," he hedged.

"Yeah. You know that's stupid, right?"

He nodded, but it didn't seem like he was willing to agree. "I have to respect my father in my business decisions. I hope you understand it's nothing personal on my part."

I shook my head and cranked the tractor ignition. It needed a minute to warm up before making the drive out to the old orchard. I raised my voice over the engine. "It became personal the moment you refused my offer when you realized a Contreras was interested in that land."

"It wasn't my decision, Selena." Conner backed away, calling his dog to his side.

"Why don't you ask your father what he's afraid of. I'm not that scary. A little healthy competition between businesses isn't going to hurt either family or this town." I downshifted the clutch and slowly crept forward. "I trust you'll see yourself out?"

"Come on, Duke." Conner whistled for his dog.

"Bye, Duke! Come visit me anytime you want, big guy." I waved at the best member of the Ashford clan as I headed down the long drive to the orchards.

Chapter Thirteen

CONNER

I almost made it out of there with most of my pride intact. Selena had the strange ability to make me feel small, even though I was a giant in this town. Even though I would head back to my thriving vineyard while she rode that piece of junk out to a bunch of trees that seemed surprised they were still bearing fruit.

I started the engine, but before I could sneak away, dust kicked up on the winding drive, signaling an oncoming car. I hoped it wasn't her brother, or worse, her father.

Lena might be stubborn in refusing to take my money, but for the first time, it hadn't felt like she despised my very presence. The rest of her family probably wouldn't be as kind.

As the dust settled, I caught sight of a familiar Ferrari as it wound around the barn to park behind it in a spot shielded from the house. Glancing toward the back door, I realized Mrs. Contreras had gone inside, and Carter was hiding his car from her.

Leaving Duke in the car, I stepped out to meet my brother. He gave me a skeptical look when he climbed out. His curls looked more unruly than normal. Sometimes, I wondered if he reveled in his messy look. I used the think he just didn't care, but maybe it was his way to fight against our more put-together family.

"What are you doing here?" He slid his sunglasses into his hair.

"I could ask you the same thing." I crossed my arms. "Aren't you supposed to only meet Lena in secret spots you think none of us know about?" My father was going to force Carter into a corner executive office one of these days, and he wouldn't be able to spend all his afternoons hanging out in a decrepit orchard.

A smile tilted his lips. "Just here to see my girl. Don't worry, I'm used to evading her family. Once she sees I'm here, she'll sneak away."

His girl. Selena. I stared at him, trying to figure him out, and then he laughed.

"Relax, bro." He clapped me on the shoulder as he walked by. "I very much doubt I'm here for the same reason as you."

Something in his laughter told me he didn't mean the check that now burned a hole in my pocket, but he was already walking toward the dirt lane through the trees Lena had disappeared down.

I slid into the car, and Duke stuck his head between the two front seats, nudging my shoulder. I rubbed his nose absently as I realized what an idiot I was. I'd come here to pay Lena for being kind. She and Carter would probably have a good laugh about it.

But unlike my brother, money was the only way I knew how to do things.

And money didn't win with people like Selena Contreras. I'd tried doing a nice thing, tried mending some of the rift. She and Enzo didn't have to help us, their rivals, the people actively trying to hold them back.

And yet, they had.

So, why couldn't I do the same? Why couldn't I help her secure the land? It wasn't that I didn't want to, but I had so little control. I'd never really noticed how much of the business truly wasn't under my power until now. It would be many years before it was.

And until then, there was nothing I could do to change my father.

That sudden thought sent a wave of anger ripping through me. My hands clenched around the steering wheel as I pulled away from the property. There was only one place where I had any control.

Parking at the Ashford property, I let Duke out and slammed the door. "Go run, buddy." He wouldn't leave the expansive grounds, and I wasn't in the mood for company. Not even his.

Duke loped off down the grassy hill, and I marched toward the barn that had become my sanctuary. I wasn't capable of many things, something I'd learned recently, and I had little power, but inside these walls, I was king.

I didn't let anyone else work with me in here, even cleaning the equipment myself. Carter once joked it was the only time I ever cleaned anything with my own two hands. He was one to talk.

I ran my fingers over one of the stainless steel wine tanks I used for the aging process. Some wines also aged in oak barrels, both American oak and French oak. Each added a different flavor profile. The oak barrels could never be fully cleaned of previous wines, and had a shorter shelf life, but they transferred their own unique flavor into the wine.

I didn't have to replace the stainless steel tanks nearly as often, and they let me have more control over how much air reached the wine.

Right now in each of the tanks, I had a batch I'd pressed from hybrid grapes I found on a recent trip to Milan. The fermentation was nearly complete, and once it sat a bit longer, I would start adding external flavors.

I stepped up to the cluttered desk at the back of the room and flipped the page on the notebook that served as my wine bible. My collection of notebooks held the data on every experiment I'd ever conducted. Every batch of wine I made went into this book. A few of them were added into the Ashford exports, others sold in small, exclusive batches.

But there were many more that would never again see the light of day.

Here, in this room, no one saw my failures except me. They didn't know I made many more undrinkable wines than any worthy of consumption. Or that I was okay with that. It was the purpose of trying new things.

My anger toward the rest of my life didn't make it past the door with me. There was no room for it in here. I scanned my latest notes, getting excited it was about time to test different flavors with the batch sitting behind me in the tanks. The wine inside was about six months old at this point.

I reached onto a shelf to pull down an acid test kit and a jar of honey so I could increase the alcohol content of one of the tanks, a practice prohibited in much of the commercial wine-making world, unless I was running a winery in France.

Lucky for me, I planned to hold one of these tanks back for mostly personal use and gifts rather than selling it.

I was about to open one of the oak barrels when I heard a car door slam outside.

"Hello?" a voice called.

My father wasn't in residence today, having gone on a short trip to visit with a few clients in upstate New York. He'd return tomorrow. But the house was fully staffed.

"Anyone here?"

I sighed, recognizing the voice. Setting my supplies down

on the desk, I wiped my hands and walked from the barn to find Conrad on his knees with Duke practically mauling him.

But I knew my brother loved it.

He hadn't come alone. Red hung back, watching Duke suspiciously, his ears tilted forward. I always found it a bit off-putting that my older brother had a fox as a pet, but he had the temperament of a cat, and Conrad was odder than most.

"Look who came off their island to see his family." I smiled as I walked toward him. I'd seen Conrad a few days ago on the boat, but before then, sightings were pretty rare, especially at our family home.

Conrad straightened and tapped his leg. Red stepped forward and leaned against it, his tail flicking and his eyes never leaving Duke.

"Jasper called." It was then I noticed Conrad hiked a bag up on his shoulder.

Jasper was in charge of the estate's stables. "Something wrong with one of the horses?"

Conrad gave me a strange look. "You live here, shouldn't you know?"

I shrugged. Horses weren't really my thing. Not anymore. When I was younger, I rode every day the weather allowed, but that passion was lost among the business of the vineyards and the winery.

Conrad rolled his eyes. "Dad's not here, is he?"

"No, he's out of town."

"Small mercies." Ever since Conrad stepped away from the family, forsaking his role within the Ashford empire to live at the Corolla Sanctuary, surrounded only by wild horses and his pet fox, our father refused to talk to him.

I hadn't ever told Conrad this, but I envied him in a way. He'd found his life's purpose—protecting and caring for animals—and here I was, working for the family business.

"Jasper should be in the main stables." I walked with Conrad up the pathway to the state-of-the-art stables where we housed well-bred horses that were more of an investment than anything else. Conrad didn't need me to go with him, he knew the way, but I kept walking.

We hadn't been close since we were kids. There was always something different about the second Ashford brother. He and our sister, now a college student, had bonded over things like bucking the family and their shared love of the horses while Carter and I had a different sort of understanding.

Conrad didn't have a vet practice in town, yet he was still the man we called, the one our stable hands trusted when something went wrong.

We'd almost reached the stable when Conrad cleared his throat. "So, that was some day out on the yacht."

I couldn't help laughing at the way he said it, like he still couldn't believe it had happened. "Yeah, who'd have thought four Ashford boys could be so useless? I just wish we hadn't had to rely on Lena and Enzo for help."

Conrad grunted. "That again?"

"What?"

He shook his head. "Careful, brother, your father is showing."

"What's that supposed to mean?"

He opened the stable door, and the smell of hay hit us in full force. "Just … don't be him. Don't carry this stupid feud on into another generation."

I didn't get a chance to respond as Jasper walked toward us. "It's Belle. I think she has colic."

I wasn't sure which horse was Belle, but Conrad didn't seem to have that issue, leaving me with Red as he led Jasper past a dozen full stalls to get to one on the end.

Red looked up at me, his eyes boring into mine, and I got the feeling the fox saw way too much. I turned and walked out of the barn, wondering where Duke had gone off to. He hadn't followed us to the stables, but he'd probably found a good place to sleep—away from Red.

Being around the fox made him as uneasy as it made me.

I groaned when Red followed on my heels. "Go back to Conrad."

He didn't listen, trailing me to the wooden fence I leaned against to wait for Conrad. The hot sun beat down on me, and I wiped sweat from my forehead.

Still, the fox stared.

"No wonder Duke doesn't like you." I glared at him. "Stop looking at me."

He inched closer.

"I can feel your gaze, Red." Wow, I really had lost my mind. Standing in the paddock talking to a fox. I rubbed my brow. "Your eyes are creepy."

I tried my best to ignore him as I waited. Conrad came out a little while later, and Red hadn't moved.

My brother, the traitor, laughed. "He likes to freak people out with the staring."

"I can see that."

Conrad walked past me. I stepped up beside him and kept pace. "Was it colic?" I didn't know exactly what colic was.

Conrad shook his head. "An infection. I gave Jasper a formula he'll need to pick up from the compounder, but Belle will be fine."

"That's good."

"I have a few minutes before I need to leave to catch the ferry back to Corolla. Want me to give Duke a checkup while I'm here?"

"Might as well. It's been a while since he's been in to the vet."

We rounded the barn that held my lab—for want of a better name—and I scanned the lawns for Duke. He was nowhere to be found.

"Duke!" I called.

"Where would he have gone?" Conrad asked.

"There are a few places he hides so I won't bother him when he sleeps."

Conrad laughed. "Smart dog."

"Too smart."

We searched everywhere I could think of around the property. Duke only went into the vineyards with me, and I wasn't sure where else he could be.

I tried calling for him one final time, but he didn't come loping around the corner like I expected.

Conrad left for the ferry with Red, but I didn't stop looking. I couldn't.

Because I refused to believe Duke was gone.

Chapter Fourteen
LENA

"No, Enzo, I'm not done yet." The bucket started to sink just as I was pruning the top of the last tree of the day. The sun was sitting low on the horizon and sweat ran down my back, but we'd made good time, and the pruning tower had held out just fine.

"That wasn't me," Enzo called from the ground below. "We're losing pressure again." He moved to fiddle with the hydraulic settings for the lift, but I was still sinking slowly to the ground. "Ugh, why can't anything on this farm work like it's supposed to?"

"It's no biggie." Enzo shrugged. "We'll work on it tonight, and it'll be fine by morning."

"Just for once, I wish we could get our work done with dependable equipment." And if I could ever get the loan I needed to buy the expensive property I wanted, I was going to replace some of the dinosaurs we were working with. Most girls dreamed of expensive dresses and shoes. Not me. I dreamed about top of the line harvesting equipment and a brand new apple press.

"I'll get the ladders from the truck." Enzo left me hanging

ten feet off the ground in the tiny pruning bucket.

"Enzo! Get me down first!" I stood with my hands on my hips as he laughed his way down the line of trees to the truck.

My phone vibrated in my pocket with the call I'd been expecting for two days.

"Eli." I stared at the lawyer's name on the screen, too scared to answer it. We didn't get good cell service way out here. "Hello?" my voice shook as I answered. "Eli? Can you hear me?" The line was garbled. "I'll call you right back!" I ended the call, hoping he heard me. It was nearing five o'clock, and Eli was quick to call it a day. He wouldn't answer work calls once he left the office.

I was still sinking, but a good seven feet from the ground. I opened the bucket door and sat on the floor, dangling my legs over the side. Scooting forward until I was hanging from the bucket, I finally let go, dropping to the ground like a sack of apples. "Ouch!" I rolled over onto my back and struggled for breath.

"Lena, what are you doing? I was coming right back." Enzo dropped the ladder and jogged to help me up from the ground.

"The loan." I clutched his arm. "Eli called."

"Go!" He handed me the truck keys and shoved me forward. "I'll finish and meet you back at the barn."

I ran, sliding into the front seat and fumbling with the ignition. "Eli, you better not leave early." I put the truck in gear and hit the gas, kicking up dirt behind me. It was a quick trip back to the barn, but my heart was pounding by the time three bars on my phone lit up, and the call finally went through.

"Eli? Glad I caught you." I took a deep breath, hoping for a miracle, because that was what it would take to secure the funds to buy the land at a price the Ashfords wouldn't be able to say no to. Still, I had to try.

"I'm sorry, Lena." Eli sighed into the phone. "The bank denied your loan application."

"Oh." My shoulders sank right along with my heart. "Well …" I ran a shaky hand through my dusty hair. "We knew it was a long shot. I just thought putting my half of Orchard Hill up as collateral would be enough. It's everything I have."

"I'm afraid the loan officer said Orchard Hill didn't appraise at the value we were expecting, though she did say your plans for the future were remarkable and potentially a great opportunity for the right investor."

"I don't want to deal with investors." I sighed. I wanted to keep it in the family and do this my way.

"I know it's not the news you wanted, but you know I'm going to help you get this thing done."

"I know, and I appreciate all you've done." I wouldn't have made it this far without him, even if he was an Ashford. He was a good one.

"You know what our next steps need to be, don't you?" I could hear the hesitation in his voice. He didn't want this any more than I did.

"It's not ideal, but I don't see another option. We'll start looking for other locations outside of Superiore Bay next week."

"It's a sad loss for the town, but it's your best alternative if you don't want to bring in local investors. Try to have a good night, Lena. It's not the end of your dreams, just a temporary setback."

"Thanks, Eli." I ended the call just as a tear splashed against my hand. It felt like the end of everything. Three years of planning and saving every spare dollar I could, just to see it all come crashing down around me because the Ashfords wanted to hold me back. All for the sake of a feud that had absolutely nothing to do with me or any of the Contrerases living today.

I wondered if Conner and the old man knew just how pathetic they were. I climbed out of the truck and headed for the barn. I didn't want to see anyone yet. I didn't want to see my mother's relief or my father's *I told you so* look when they heard the news that it was likely over.

I kicked a bale of hay in the entryway and headed to the back stall to sulk in private. Sure, I could probably find another land parcel in another town that would work well enough. I just didn't know if I could get as excited for the future as I was when I saw my family bringing Orchard Hill to the tourists and locals of Superiore Bay. It was a way for us to give back to the town that had given us so much. To take our business to one of the neighboring towns felt like the ultimate betrayal.

"Hi, Sweet Floof." I sank to the hay covered floor, scooping up the white mama cat that called the barn her home. She ruled over the barn like a queen, keeping it free of mice and other cats who thought to take up residence here. She was heavily pregnant with a new litter of kittens, but she purred, bumping her head against my chin and giving me her compassionate blue-eyed gaze. "Oh, Sweets." I buried my face in her fur and let the tears fall. "What am I going to do now?"

For three years, I had something I was working toward. A future I could be proud of—not that I wasn't proud of my family's accomplishments with Orchard Hill as it was. I just … wanted more for our future. With the loan denied, I didn't know if there would ever be anything more to look forward to. Life would go on just as it always had, and nothing would change.

A familiar bark sent me creeping into the shadows of the stall. The very last person I wanted to see right now was Conner Ashford and his sweet dog. "Go away, Duke," I whispered, hoping he would heed my plea. But his barking grew closer until I heard him sniffing like a bloodhound on the trail of Conrad Ashford's adorable fox.

He turned the corner, nose to the ground, until he saw me. He leaned down, head resting on massive paws, butt wiggling in the air in the universal dog language of *do you want to play?*

"Where's your dad?" I set the cat back into her hay nest and called Duke forward. I hadn't heard a car approach, and I didn't hear any voices in the yard. "Did you come here all by yourself?"

Duke wiggled his hind end and scooted forward until his head rested in my lap. I scratched behind his ears, and his tongue lolled out as he rolled onto his back. "Do you like belly rubs?" I tickled his belly, and his eyes rolled back into his head.

"Aw, who's a good boy?" I rubbed his fuzzy belly. "But your dad's going to be looking for you." If he wasn't already. Though Orchard Hill was likely the last place Conner would come looking for his missing dog. "Maybe I'll just keep you as compensation for losing my land."

Duke gave me a wary look at that, his ears flopping back to reveal his wolfish eyes. "It's a good thing I know you're a sweet boy because I wouldn't want to run into you on a dark path in the woods."

Duke yawned, snapping his jaws, and leaned forward to sniff at Sweet Floof, who regarded him with barely concealed hostility. Duke ignored her sassy aura and moved to curl up around his new friends. With the cat snuggled up against his belly and his head resting in my lap, he made himself at home.

I snapped a quick picture. "Let's text your uncle and ask him to come get you." I sent the picture to Carter with the caption "your brother missing someone important?" at the bottom.

Three dancing dots immediately popped up on my screen, and I waited for his reply.

Carter: His dad is absolutely *freaking* out. I'll be right there.

I smiled at the thought of Conner missing his dog. I didn't want to like the guy—especially today—but it was clear he loved Duke.

"Someone with such good taste in dogs can't be all that bad." I rubbed Duke's head. "He just needs to figure out if he's going to be like his father or if he's got the strength to be his own man."

While I waited for Carter to arrive, I went in search of a treat for Duke and Sweet Floof. She didn't like apples, snooty cat that she was, but she did like peanut butter and bananas.

"Wait a second, big boy." I sat back down on the barn floor as I sliced into a Pink Lady apple, slathering it with peanut butter for Duke. He chomped it down, his tongue working hard at the peanut butter stuck to the roof of his mouth.

For Sweets, I sat a plate of banana and peanut butter for her to enjoy on her own. She wouldn't let Duke anywhere near it. "Sit, boy." I waited for Duke to comply before I fed him a second piece of apple.

"That is not the best way to ensure he doesn't show up again." My shoulders tensed at the sound of Conner's voice. Not Carter. He stuck me with his brother again?

"I know what you're thinking. In Carter's defense, he was coming straight here to get Duke, but I wouldn't let him." Conner crouched beside Duke, pulling him into a hug. "What do you mean running away on me like that, huh? I was worried sick." Duke worked at the peanut butter, his tail thumping against Conner's side.

"I'm so sorry he just showed up. He's never done this before." Conner turned his attention on me, and some emotion crossed his face.

"It's okay." I stood, smoothing a hand over my hair. I must look like a mess. "He can come visit anytime."

"Thanks for looking out for him." Conner moved to sit on an overturned bucket, making himself at home just like his dog had.

All I wanted was for him to leave me alone to lick my wounds in peace. "What are you doing, Conner?"

Chapter Fifteen

CONNER

What *was* I doing? I'd come to get my errant dog, but I couldn't tear him away from the treats he seemed to be enjoying so much.

That was definitely my reason for hanging around the barn with the one person who probably never wanted to see me again.

Right?

I refused to think anything was going on with me, so instead I focused on something else. "That cat is pregnant."

"Yeah?" Lena rolled her eyes. "I hadn't noticed, what with it being so obvious and all."

I wanted to get angry at her tone, but instead I smiled. She leaned back against a stall door, seemingly not caring that she was sitting on the dirty ground. Her overalls—an odd choice of clothing for a grown woman—were streaked with dirt that told me she must have been working outside since I saw her a few hours ago. One of the buckles was undone, leaving the top of the overalls hanging haphazardly over her pale blue t-shirt.

As she lifted a hand to run her fingers through her messy

hair, I noticed a hole in the armpit of the shirt. This girl was a mess.

She pulled her hand back with a grimace and looked at it. It was only then I noticed she had peanut butter on her fingers and now in her hair. She wiped the rest off on her pants.

A laugh rumbled out of me, and she narrowed her eyes. I was past the point of overstaying my welcome now, not like I'd been welcome in the first place. "Duke likes you." I couldn't hide my surprise. Duke liked lots of people he knew and trusted, but he didn't curl up against their legs and rest his head on their laps. Other than me, he was mostly standoffish with strangers, wanting to be scratched and then left to his own devices.

"Doesn't sound like you approve." She dug her hands into his fur, and he closed his eyes. *Traitor.*

I watched the two of them, noticing the sad tilt of Lena's shoulders, the way she stared at Duke like she needed his presence. Maybe that was why I was still here. I couldn't take him away from her when she looked so … sad. Was she sad?

The thought didn't sit well with me. I'd always known Lena to be combative, capable, strong to the point of irritating most of the time. Definitely not sad.

A sigh wound through her, and her shoulders sank lower. Her head fell back against the wooden stall door behind her. "I still don't know why you're here, Conner. I'm really not in the mood for our nasty banter today." Something in the way she looked at me told me she blamed me for whatever had happened.

I pursed my lips. "You're mean."

A harsh laugh escaped her. "Excuse me?"

"To me. I don't understand why you hate me so much, yet you adore Carter."

"I don't *adore* Carter. Who even says that? He's my friend. I care about him."

"But he's an Ashford too." What made Carter so different? Why had she decided our families' fight extended to me and not him?

"Yeah, he's an Ashford, but he doesn't treat me like I'm any less than him."

My brow furrowed. "Lena …"

"Besides, you're the one who is mean. Not me."

I'd admit I struggled to contain my meaner impulses sometimes, but I wanted to be different. "I'm sorry."

She laughed again. "You're sorry? That's rich coming from you."

"What does that mean?"

She pulled her hand back from Duke, not answering me. The cat stood, arching her back as she stretched. She stepped onto Lena's legs that were crossed like a pretzel, turned around once, and lay down.

Duke wiggled across the small space between him and Lena. His long tongue drooped out of his mouth. Giving the cat one slobbery lick, he rested his head on Lena's knee. I watched the animals' rearrangement with fascination.

The woman who'd fought with me in town, the one who'd pushed me into the bay, hadn't seemed like someone who'd garner such affection from the most honest of creatures. Yet, something drew them to her.

"Why are you staring at me?" She cocked her head to the side, studying me. Her earnest gaze sent a wave of discomfort over me, and I shifted, trying to keep my balance on the uncomfortable bucket.

"It's just … Duke … he ran from me and came to you."

"And?" She scratched his head. "We're friends." A laugh that sounded slightly less sad escaped her. "Are you really that upset he came here?"

"Not really." It was the truth. "I'm more upset that he left our property at all. I don't like the idea of him wandering Superiore Bay on his own."

"Well, what was different?"

"What do you mean?"

"Something made him want to get away."

I thought for a moment. She was right. Something had been different. "Red was there."

"Red? That a codename for a girl or—"

"My brother's fox."

She smiled at that, but there was still a heaviness to it. "Ah, well, that would do it. I imagine he doesn't like the fox. I've seen Conrad in town with him." She leaned down to talk to Duke. "I find a pet fox a bit eerie too, boy."

He opened one eye and then closed it with a body-heaving sigh.

Something was still bothering me. "Why didn't you accept my apology?"

Her smile fell away, and she busied herself stroking the cat. Loud purring filled the space between us. "I wasn't exactly sure which thing you're sorry for."

"Are there really that many things?"

"Yes." She gently moved the cat from her lap and stood, wiping off her pants. It was no use, there was no getting them clean. "Now, I love Duke being here, but really, Conner, you should keep better track of your dog. It's a long walk from the Ashford Estates to here."

The way she said estates left a sour taste in my mouth. I felt very much like I was being dismissed. Duke stood up, bending forward with his butt in the air to stretch. He followed Lena toward the door of the barn, sparing no look for me.

I walked after them, watching as she stepped into the early evening light. It reflected off her dark hair, casting her in a glow. She took a deep breath as if fortifying herself.

I didn't see Enzo approaching until he'd almost reached us.

His eyes narrowed as he looked from her to me to the barn we'd just exited. I knew Enzo was younger than Lena, but he acted like a protective older brother.

"What are you doing here, Ashford?" Gone was the helpful man who'd diagnosed the problem with our boat and towed us to the marina. I was on his territory now.

Before I could answer, Lena spoke. "Duke ran away and came here. Conner was just picking him up." Her eyes drifted to me. "And leaving."

I nodded.

Enzo, seemingly satisfied with that explanation, focused all his attention on Lena. "I was expecting you to come back and tell me the news."

She gave a slight shake of her head, and the hopeful expression on Enzo's face fell. "Well, okay, we'll look at other options."

"Not now, Enzo. We'll talk about it later."

I could take a hint, yet my feet didn't move.

Enzo ignored me and kept his focus on his sister. "I want to finish up the section we were working on before coming in for dinner. Mom made chili."

The corners of Lena's lips lifted slightly. "That sounds heavenly right now. I'll be out to help you in just a minute. I was going to grab Sweets some fresh water first."

Enzo rolled his eyes to me. "Stupid name for a cat, right?"

I only shrugged.

He put a hand on Lena's shoulder. "We'll figure something out, okay?"

I got the feeling he was talking about whatever news Lena had delivered to him with one shake of her head, whatever news had made her sad. I wanted to know what it was, to know if I could help, but I wasn't Carter. Lena and I weren't friends.

Without a backward glance, Enzo walked toward the tidy rows of trees in the distance.

Lena waited a few beats before turning to me. "Thanks for coming to get Duke. I don't think he'd have fit on my moped for me to drive him home."

I looked pointedly at the rusted truck, knowing she had other ways to get around. She just didn't like them. Lena didn't seem to notice.

I patted my leg. "Come on, Duke. Time to get out of Lena's way."

Duke didn't budge from her side.

Lena crouched down, putting her hands on each side of his face. "You're never in my way, boy, but you have to go home with your dad."

He looked up at me, his eyes holding a silent accusation. *I know, boy,* I thought. *I want to stay too.* I wasn't sure where that thought came from, but it didn't go away.

This place was so different from the atmosphere at home where I mostly only spoke with servants. My grandfather was around, and I appreciated that, but I ate most of my meals sitting at the desk in my barn-office. Working. There were no family dinners with homemade chili.

Our cook prepared our food, but it wasn't the same as when my mom had been around. She'd have liked it here too if the Ashfords had been allowed on the property. The stifling quality of our life hadn't suited her.

I wasn't sure what it was about this place that brought her to mind. Maybe it was that she'd always dreamed of her kids getting along, of us being each other's best friends. But what Lena had with Enzo, I'd never had.

Sure, I loved all three of my siblings. But Conrad was absent most of the time, Carter fought so hard against family expectations I got caught up in his view of the enemy, and Jorgina was so much younger than me I hardly knew her. She was away at college, and we never spoke on the phone. It was like she was a stranger who shared my last name.

It had never made me sad before, but now, for some reason, I had to urge the talk to her.

"Go on, Duke." Lena gestured toward me and my sparkling Mercedes that looked so out of place among the dusty roads, rusty equipment, and apple trees.

Duke finally relented and returned to my side. I didn't like not having him there. We'd been a pair for too long. He was my truest friend, and I wondered if that made me pitiful. Suddenly, I couldn't leave while Lena and I were still at odds.

I stopped at my car, tapping a knuckle against the dark paint, and turned. Lena was still there, waiting for me to leave.

"Can we call a truce?" I blurted.

"A what?" She didn't laugh at me like I'd half expected. Instead, curiosity rose in her gaze.

"A truce. Sign a peace treaty. Whatever you want to call it. I'm tired, Lena. So tired of being told I have to hate people I hardly even know. I don't want to hate you anymore or fight with you." As I said the words, I knew I still couldn't give her what she wanted. I couldn't sell the land without my father.

My grandfather's words came back to me, and I realized I didn't want her to fail. That wasn't the kind of person I wanted to be.

Slowly, agonizingly slowly, Lena nodded. "A truce. Okay. No more fights in front of the entire town?"

My lips quirked up. "No more trips into the bay."

She stuck out her hand. "Deal."

I clasped her hand, feeling her warmth wind through me. Something wet hit me, and I looked down to see Duke lick our clasped hands. Lena laughed as she pulled her hand back and wiped it on her pants. "This doesn't mean we're friends, though, right?"

Friends. It was such a foreign word.

"Definitely not."

Yet, when we shared a final smile, it felt like maybe that was possible. I got it now. Why Carter kept coming back to her despite threats from his family. Lena was special. But more than that, the thought of having a friend, having someone who actually cared, meant more than any of our trust funds ever could.

Chapter Sixteen

LENA

Superiore Bay was going to hate me.

There were three things the people of this town detested. Hidden gossip—they preferred to know it all. Hidden allegiances—Superiore Bay or die. And Hidden Cove—the town next door with an even bigger stretch of coast than us. They'd been our rivals as long as I could remember.

Our businesses fought for superiority, our town councils fought for tourists, and our high schools fought for sports supremacy. Hidden Cove was no trouble when it came to sports. We always won. But tourists … well, they had more beaches than we did. The Ashford's vineyards and winery brought people to town, as did our orchard, but neither compared to the gorgeous beaches, boat tours, and the Hidden Point Lighthouse.

Basically, the residents of Hidden Cove considered us second rate.

But what they also had plenty of? Land. And the town council attracted new businesses with tax cuts and grants, something Superiore Bay didn't have the money or available land to do.

I stared at my computer screen as an icon circled. Our internet was ridiculously slow, but it was all we could get out at the orchard. The page finally pulled up. I looked around my parents' kitchen, making sure no one was around, before diving into the information on Hidden Cove.

If the Ashfords wouldn't sell me the land at a reasonable price, I had to look elsewhere. I wasn't ready to give up my dream. There was another reason Hidden Cove was the logical place to look. Investors.

I wanted to do this myself, but the reality was, I might never get approved for a business loan. No matter how cheap I could get the land, it wouldn't matter if I couldn't get the funds.

And investors flocked to the tourist haven, all wanting a piece of their summer dollars.

I had an email sitting in my inbox right now from someone who'd gotten my name from Eli. A young investor looking to make his first splash. That was how he'd put it. I could tell his youth from the way he talked in his email. He was likely around my age and had some of Daddy's money to put to use.

I'd stared at the email long into last night when I should have been sleeping to prepare for another exhausting day at the orchard. I hadn't expected my grandmother to notice how tired I was and demand I take the day off.

So, now, my dad was out picking up my slack, and I felt awful about it.

But not as awful as I'd feel once the town found out what I was considering.

The Hidden Cove official website had a listing of land and properties for sale. I'd already made a few calls and had my first appointment in one hour. I slammed the lid of my laptop harder than I intended and looked up to find my grandmother watching me.

"What did that computer ever do to you?"

I wasn't telling the rest of the family about my meetings in Hidden Cove. They wouldn't understand what I was willing to do to make this happen. Not even Enzo would approve of me looking outside Superiore Bay. He'd been the football captain in high school and never gotten free of that rivalry.

But Gram was different.

I sighed, leaning back in my chair. "I'm meeting with an investor today." I paused. "In Hidden Cove."

The condemnation I'd expect from anyone else didn't come. Instead, she sat across from me. "I'm proud of you."

"Why? For taking the easy route?"

Gram shook her head. "There is nothing easy about this path you've chosen. But you're willing to fight for what you want. Forget town rivalries, you're swallowing your pride by taking that meeting. And pride has no place in business or in dreams. Sometimes, we need to sacrifice our stubbornness, our desire to do everything on our own."

"Gram, what if this man ... what if he doesn't see my vision?"

"There's no law saying you must take his money if you don't see eye to eye. It's just a meeting."

"I know." I blew out a breath. "I should get going."

She nodded. "Don't let anyone try to dictate how you achieve your dreams, *Mija*. As long as you have a foundation of strong values, determination, and a desire to affect change for the better, you'll be fine."

Leave it to my grandmother to choose those as her tenants of solid business decisions. I couldn't say she was wrong. I wanted to do something good for this town, but if that wasn't possible, I still wanted to do something good. It was only the location that changed.

I walked out of the house, stopping in my tracks as I caught sight of Enzo and Carter huddled together near the barn. I started toward them, hearing their whispers but not making out their words.

My foot scuffed on the ground, and they both turned to me, looking like they'd been caught with their hand in the proverbial cookie jar. My eyes narrowed. "Hey guys." As far as I knew, they weren't friends. Enzo may have been nicer about it, but he'd warned me away from Carter, just as Carter's brother warned him. They didn't think our friendship was worth inflaming the families.

My eyes shifted from my brother to my friend and back again. They were up to something. I could tell. And when either of them were plotting on their own, it spelled trouble. Together ...

But I didn't have time for this. "Enzo, shouldn't you be working?"

"Si, *hermana*." He scurried off. But now, I was even more suspicious. Enzo didn't often pull out the Spanish, not like our parents and grandmother. It was a distraction, meant to make me think he was just being affectionate.

I shook off my suspicion and turned to Carter. "You're driving."

"Sure." He walked to his car and opened the door for me. "Where are we going?"

"Hidden Cove."

"Do I want to ask?"

I sighed as I sank into the leather seat, wishing this car wasn't so small. I felt it closing in around me. Carter cranked the engine, and it roared to life, way louder than it needed to be. He grinned as he took off down the drive.

We reached the main drag that would take us out of town by the time I answered him. "I'm about to become a traitor to Superiore Bay by considering another town for my business."

"So, I'm the accomplice?"

"Pretty much."

"Well, being that it's my family forcing you to look elsewhere for land, it's fitting you bring me down with you."

"Glad you see it that way."

We shared a smile before he turned back to the road. I hung my arm out the window, letting the rush of air blow strands of hair loose from my braid. I'd be a mess by the time I got to this meeting, but that wasn't anything new for me.

Reaching into Carter's glove box, I retrieved the sunglasses I always kept in there and relaxed to enjoy the short drive up the coast. Superiore Bay faded behind us, and it wasn't long before Hidden Cove materialized, its main town center more pristine than ours. It lacked the character I loved Superiore Bay for, built more for tourists than the enjoyment of the people living there year round.

Tourist shops lined Main Street, selling everything from useless trinkets and t-shirts to chocolate. Chocolate was their claim to fame, boasting of the largest chocolatier in the state. The income the family who owned it generated rivaled that of the Ashfords.

I'd never tell anyone in Superiore Bay this, but I'd rather our town sell chocolate than wine.

We drove through town to the address I'd written down of the first property. It was on the far side, but near the center of things. The location was perfect. I wasn't sure about the small size. It might work for our first phase, but any growth would be constrained.

Carter dutifully drove me to each of the properties on my list before I told him there was something I needed in town. I hadn't yet mentioned the investor.

Carter parked in a lot and cut the engine. "I forgot how much I love this town." He eyed me. "Don't you dare tell anyone back home I said that."

I let loose a smile. "You just like how there's a chocolate shop on every corner."

"Speaking of … will you be fine on your own for an hour or so? A buddy of mine works in town, and I wanted to stop over and see him."

"What friend of yours don't I know?"

He shrugged but didn't answer as he got out of the car. I followed him, relieved I wouldn't have to tell him about the investor until I knew more. "Sure, I'll head over and grab some lunch at the diner."

Carter and I went our separate ways, and I walked to the familiar diner, stepping inside as a bell rang above the door. It hadn't changed, and I soaked it in. In high school, during the summers, Carter and I would sneak over to Hidden Cove with our friend Harper. It was the only way to escape the eyes of the town and our families who didn't want us spending time together.

A long counter sat in a semi-circle in the front with glass ketchup bottles spaced out along with silverware and napkins. A scattering of tables were full of hungry patrons eating their lunches.

An older woman walked toward me. "Hello, dear. Can I help you with something?"

"I'm meeting someone here. His name is Colin."

"Ah." She smiled. "Colin. Yes, he said he had a meeting. He's right over there." She pointed to a table in the corner where an attractive young man sat looking at his phone.

I stopped at the edge of the table. "Colin Walker?"

He looked up like he was surprised to hear his name. "Oh, yeah. Colin Walker. That's me."

I sat tentatively. "You don't sound too sure of that."

He slid his phone away and fixed dazzling green eyes on me. His blond hair was shaved on the sides but long on top, looking both professional and not. He wore khaki shorts and a navy blue polo, seeming more ready for the golf course than a business meeting.

"Okay," he said. "I'm not Colin Walker. I gave that name because you wouldn't meet with me if you knew who I really was."

I lifted an eyebrow, trying to keep my irritation in check. "I knew this would be a waste of time." I stood but stopped when his hand shot out to grab my wrist.

"I'm Colin Hillson."

A Hillson. Just perfect. "The only thing worse than an Ashford is a Hillson," I mumbled. At least the Ashfords were from the right town.

"What?" His lips quirked up.

"Nothing. Please let me go."

"I'm sorry I lied." He removed his hand. "But Eli sent me some information about your plans, and I was intrigued."

"Why would Eli do that?"

"For you, I assume. I've known him since Harvard. Look, I'm going to be honest, I don't want to work with someone from Superiore Bay any more than you want to work with me, but I'm trying to bring something big to this town, something that will show my father I can succeed on my own. And I think your plans are it."

The chocolate empire must not be any different from the wine business if they too were losing sons.

I didn't want to listen to what he had to say, but I wasn't sure I had any other options at this point. Even if it meant getting put in the middle of another argument between a powerful man and his children, I needed his money.

I slid back into my seat. "No more lies. I'll listen to your proposal for bringing the business to Hidden Cove at the very least." I crossed my arms, wishing I was anywhere else.

All I knew was if anyone in Superiore Bay found out I'd

even set foot in the same room as Colin Hillson, there'd be a reckoning.

The hair on the back of my neck prickled, and I glanced out the window, feeling like I was being watched, but there was no one there.

I rubbed my eyes as I listened to Colin speak, but the sensation didn't go away.

Chapter Seventeen
CONNER

Something was up.

Superiore Bay was a rather nosey town. It was something everyone who grew up here got used to. There was a particular interest in my family, the antics of my brothers and my cousins.

The *Weekly Wine* was a town icon, the newspaper designed to share town gossip.

But this time, it held something more serious. I could tell.

I was sitting in the town square, steps away from the gazebo, where a ring of the town's worst gossipers congregated in the mornings. They were the old lady crew, a band of retired women who spent their summers hanging out in the park, never alone.

They'd always kind of scared me a bit, mostly because they were the only people in town who didn't give me deference.

"Conner! Conner Ashford." A woman shuffled my way, and I looked up, relieved it was Mrs. Chapman and not her counterparts. I wasn't in the mood for the overt flirting I normally got from Mrs. Peterson and Mrs. Jeffries.

I grimaced, taking note of the copy of the *Weekly Wine* she waved in the air. "Have you seen it?"

I sighed, realizing I should have taken the time to pick up a copy this morning before braving town. Setting my coffee down on the table next to the documents I'd been reading, I stood. Sometimes, I stopped in the town square after meetings to catch my breath, to get some space before going back to the main offices, where my father would demand every moment of my time. I was still working, just without him breathing down my neck.

"Morning, Mrs. Chapman."

She frowned. Mrs. Chapman was a formidable woman. "You haven't bothered to read the news today, have you?"

"It's not news if it's in the *Weekly Wine*. It's gossip."

She waved away my words and slapped the paper down on top of my folder of documents. "This time, it's news."

I sighed. She wasn't going to go away until I read it.

"Look at the sightings section," she said.

I flipped the page, my eyes drifting to the column that usually made at least some mention of one of the Ashford boys. But it wasn't about us.

The headline read "Selena Contreras, Sleeping With the Enemy?" My throat tightened, and I wasn't sure I wanted to know more. But I couldn't stop myself.

The short paragraph described a wayward Lena, sneaking off to Hidden Cove, our rival town, to meet a secret date. And not just anyone. There was a picture, and I recognized the man instantly. Colin Hillson.

The Hillson family ran Hidden Cove in much the same way the Ashfords did Superiore Bay.

And Lena was dating him?

An unfamiliar feeling curled inside me, something dark and foreboding. For a moment, I realized what an intrusion of privacy it was that someone photographed them, but then my sympathy for her faded away.

Selena knew better.

Dating a Hillson was even worse than an Ashford and a Contreras being together. At least both our families wanted our town to succeed, to thrive. The Hillsons only wanted to tear us down.

"We need to fix this." Mrs. Chapman crossed her arms.

I'd almost forgotten she was there as my mind whirled with what this meant. My anger surged and I crumpled the paper in my fist. "Lena will do whatever she wants."

"I know your families have their differences, but all of us old women thought it was only a matter of time before you were joined in marriage."

The blood froze in my veins, and I stared at her. "What?"

"You know, your families. Selena and Carter have always been headed that way." She placed a hand on my arm. "I wanted you to be able to be the one to tell him before he finds out another way."

Breath entered my lungs, but it didn't stop me from feeling like I was being held underwater. The town expected me to fix this. I could see it in Mrs. Chapman's gaze.

I had to get away from her before I told her what I really thought of Lena and her stupidity in dating someone from Hidden Cove.

This town would never forgive her.

Movement across the square caught my eye. "Sorry, I have a cousin I need to deal with." I gathered my things, threw my half-full coffee in the trashcan, and jogged to where I'd just seen Max disappear into the alleyway between the coffee shop and the bookstore.

I caught up with him only to find he wasn't alone. His younger sister, Emery, was there with him. I couldn't remember the last time I'd seen my two youngest cousins.

MICHELLE MACQUEEN & ANN MAREE CRAVEN

Their dad had a falling out with mine when I was a kid, and since then, all holiday invitations had been lost in the mail.

"Shouldn't you two be in school?"

They both jerked around when they heard me. Emery looked scared, but Max lifted his chin defiantly. "What's up, Conner?"

I raised a brow. "That's what you have to say for yourself? It's the middle of the morning, Max."

"Thanks for the reminder, Dad."

I sighed and set my sights on the easier one, Emery. The two of them were twins, but more different than alike. They were sixteen, and I barely knew them. How sad was that?

Emery finally lifted her eyes to mine. "We needed a break, okay?"

"A break?"

Max nodded. "We have our game against Hidden Cove this week."

Game, now it made sense. Max was the quarterback of the football team. I'd seen him play a few times, and he was good, but he also had a tendency to let his nerves get the better of him. And the Hidden Cove Spring game was the biggest game of the year despite not counting toward the regular season.

My mind immediately went to Lena, wondering who she'd be rooting for in the game. There were three Hillson kids on the other team.

I shook thoughts of her from my head, sympathy for my cousins returning. I knew what it was like to face the pressure of being an Ashford in this town. Even worse was being the spurned Ashfords. They had the name and all the expectations that came with it without the money or the business.

Though, I had my suspicions that my grandfather made sure they were taken care of. My father didn't control all the purse strings.

From the set of Max's shoulders, I knew going back to

school wasn't what he needed. And Emery, she was the good one who never did anything wrong—unless it was for either of her brothers.

"Okay, fine. Come with me, and I'll buy you two something to eat at the diner." I wasn't sure when I'd gone soft or why I wanted to help them, but I had this new urge to be more than what everyone thought of me, to surprise people.

And it seemed like I'd succeeded because the twins looked at each other like they didn't trust what I was offering.

"You're not making us go back?" Max asked.

"Not until you've had some pie."

Emery looked at me. "But it's morning."

"And?" I gestured to the end of the alleyway. "Come on. If we get lemon meringue or apple, we can pretend we're just eating fruit."

They hustled out of the alley, and I ignored the stares of the ladies in the park. In the next *Weekly Wine*, I was sure there'd be a sighting of me helping my truant cousins. It was a good thing my father didn't read the paper.

We were about to step inside the diner when I noticed Carter heading up the street toward us.

"You guys grab a booth, I'll be right in."

They both shrugged and left me to wait for my brother.

Carter shielded his eyes from the sun and smiled when he got to me. "Was that Emery and Max I saw you with?"

I nodded, crossing my arms.

His smile widened. "Oh good. I've been meaning to chat with Emery. I have a book she might like."

"Wait a second … you read?"

Carter tried to look offended, but it didn't work while he was laughing. "Try not to look so shocked, brother. Em and I have been exchanging books for the last two years. We're both obsessed with the same fantasy author."

I hadn't even known Carter was in contact with the twins, but then, Carter and I didn't do much talking either.

He tried to push past me into the diner, but I put a hand out to stop him. "Wait …" I drew in a breath. "Did you see the *Weekly Wine?*"

"No." Carter laughed. "I never read that stuff, but what's interesting, Conner, is that apparently you do."

"No, what's interesting is your girlfriend was seen eating lunch with Colin Hillson in Hidden Cove."

Carter rolled his eyes to the sky. "I'm not sure how many times I have to tell people it's not like that with Lena."

"Maybe not with you, but now she's seeing the enemy."

"Enemy? Conner, do you hear yourself? You're spouting out headlines written by the bored people of this town. Leave it alone."

"So, you don't care? At all?" I would never believe he didn't have feelings for Lena. Why else would he defy our father time and again to see her?

Maybe for the same reason Duke ran to her. The same reason I'd stayed to talk instead of leaving the minute I found my dog. There was something about her that was impossible to dislike once she let her walls down, something compelling.

Carter sighed. "It is none of my business who she sees or doesn't see." He pushed past me and stopped with his hand on the door. "And it's none of yours."

I knew that. So, why did I feel like it was?

I followed Carter in, but he didn't go straight to the booth Max and Emery had chosen. I slid in, watching my brother walk to the back where Enzo sat, hovering over a mug of what I assumed was coffee.

Carter didn't stop at his table, but I could have sworn he dropped something onto it. A note, maybe? I rubbed my eyes. Maybe I'd imagined it.

Carter slipped into the bathroom, and I turned to my cousins, not really sure what to say.

We ordered pie and then stared at each other for too long. When Carter returned, it was like the entire diner sighed with relief at the end of the awkwardness. He immediately got them talking, and all I had to do was listen.

Listening, I could do. It was every other part of socializing I got wrong.

Even with family.

Chapter Eighteen

LENA

I walked around the corner clutching my small stash of new library books, still frowning from the strange stilted conversation I just had with Mrs. Abernathy. Normally, the local librarian was all too eager to discuss books with me, but today she was … almost rude.

I shook my head, wondering if there was something going on with her. Her behavior was unlike the sweet librarian I'd known since Grams had started taking me to the library every week when I was four.

"We're closed." Old Rusty McGreggor flipped the closed sign in the window of the Rusty Spoon before I could reach for the door.

"But it's lunchtime, Mr. McGreggor." I stood outside, completely stunned. The busy diner was packed as usual.

"We're at max capacity. Sorry, Selena." He locked the door and turned his back to me. Rusty McGreggor had never once called me anything but Lena my whole life.

"What has gotten into everyone today?" I turned toward the town square, catching sight of the Cheddar Chariot, the local food truck with the best selection of gourmet grilled cheese sandwiches and soups ever created. My stomach growled at the thought of choosing between my two favorites, and I headed across the street to join the line. There was always a line at the Cheddar Chariot.

"Hi, Mrs. Jeffries." I smiled at one of the Bay's most notorious town gossips. "You must be reading my mind, it's been ages since I had a grilled cheese fix from the Chariot." My smile fell as she harrumphed at me and turned away to mutter with her best friend, Mrs. Peterson.

Everyone in line took a step away from me, refusing to meet my gaze. "I know I don't smell, so what's the deal, guys?" I turned around in a slow circle, but no one seemed to have heard me. Then, I really did check to make sure I didn't smell. "What is going on in this town?"

"What can I get you?" Mallory Ellison leaned out the window with a smile.

"Finally, a friendly face." I smiled back at her.

"Oh, it's you." She scowled. "We're out of cheese."

"How is a grilled cheese food truck out of cheese?"

"Just ran out of everything but the Stinking Bishop, you want that?"

"That's the expensive stinky cheese, isn't it?" I sighed, letting my shoulders fall. It was a thirty-dollar sandwich I didn't want and couldn't afford even if I could get past the awful smell.

"Stuff's fifty dollars a pound." Mallory shrugged. She was the kindest person I knew, so clearly something was going on. The whole town seemed to be mad at me.

"Listen, Mallory," I pleaded. "Do you think you could find it in your heart to help a girl out on a bad day? What I really need right now is one of your amazing grilled pimento cheese sandwiches, with that apple-cherry chutney you make with *my* apples. Oh! And fresh homemade chips and cheese dip—I mean if you could double check to see if you have any left."

"I'll see what I can do." She slammed the window shut and went to make my order.

I stood glaring at all the townspeople around me. They were actively pretending like I didn't exist. I snatched my phone from my pocket and dialed Carter. He always knew what was going on in this silly town.

"Voicemail," I muttered irritably and ended the call, dialing Enzo next. He always answered when I called. By the time his voicemail picked up, I was good and mad. "Enzo, this is your sister," I snapped. "Something weird is going on in this insane town, and I know you and Carter are avoiding me, so call me back. Soon, before I really lose my temper." I didn't bother lowering my voice.

"Order's up," Mallory called from the pick-up window. I snatched my bag and stomped off across the town square to the empty gazebo. Normally, I loved the people in this town, but I also adored my alone time, which I rarely got. Trying to forget about my crappy day, I sat in the shade of the gazebo and dove into a new historical fantasy novel I'd waited six weeks to get my hands on. That was the great thing about the local library. Free books. I couldn't afford to feed my reading habit any other way. And when I couldn't make it to the library to chat with Mrs. Abernathy, I could download all the eBooks I wanted from the library's app.

I reached into my bag to find Mallory had done me wrong. So. Wrong. She'd filled my bag with cold, stale chips, and she'd *forgotten* my cheese dip. But she got my sandwich right. I took a huge bite of warm gooey grilled cheese and crunched into something that was not apple-cherry chutney.

"Pickles? Gross." Pickles had no business being on a grilled cheese sandwich, and Mallory knew how I felt about pickles. Well and truly angry now, I tried to pick the pickles off the sandwich and made a mess of it. "Ugh." I finally gave up and went back to my book, but even a trip back to the seventeenth-century American frontier couldn't do it for me.

I tried dialing Carter again, but he wasn't answering. Before I could think better of it, I dialed Conner's number, hoping Carter was with him.

"Conner Ashford," he answered in a bored business-man tone.

"Let me talk to Carter. Is he with you?" I tapped my foot on the gazebo floor.

"Who is this?"

"It's Lena. I need to speak with your stupid brother, but he's not answering my calls because he knows I'm mad."

"And why are you calling me again?" He sounded amused.

"Because you're his brother."

"Unfortunately, I can't help you. It's a work day, which means Carter is nowhere near the offices at the moment."

"Of course." I sighed, about to end the call.

"Why are you mad?" I could hear the creak of his desk chair. It sounded like he'd put his feet up on his desk. I could just imagine him in some snooty corner office suite, dressed in a suit that cost more than I was worth.

"I don't know." I ran a hand through my hair, not really sure why I was still talking to Conner Ashford.

"You don't know why you're mad, but you know it's Carter's fault?" There he went, sounding amused again.

"It's nothing. Something weird is going on in town, and he won't answer my calls. Sorry I bothered you." I tried to hang up again, but he stopped me.

"Yeah, you should probably ask your new boyfriend about that. I'm guessing my brother isn't answering your calls because he's hurt." Gone was his amused tone. He sounded more like an Ashford again.

"What are you even talking about, Ashford? What new

boyfriend?" Today was some kind of *Black Mirror* day. Everyone around had lost their minds.

"Carter's probably off licking his wounds. Just leave him alone, Selena." The line went dead, and I stared at the screen, at a loss for words. There was only one thing to do. I needed a copy of the *Weekly Wine*. Immediately.

I grabbed my things and darted across the street to the A Likely Story bookshop and picked up a copy from the stand out front. Walking back to the gazebo, I flipped through the gossip rag that passed for the Bay's newspaper.

Then, I saw it. A photo, taken anonymously, of course, of me dining with Colin Hillson in Hidden Cove. The caption read, "Local girl crosses the line in a romantic dalliance with the enemy."

"Oh, for Pete's sake!" I sat back down in the shade of the gazebo, fuming. Everyone *had* lost their minds if they thought I was dating Colin Hillson.

"It's time for some tough love, honey."

I jumped at the voice right behind me.

"Mrs. Chapman, you scared me to death." I laid a hand over my heart, willing it to stop racing.

"Scoot over, Lena." Mrs. Jeffries dropped down next to me, also scaring the life out of me.

"You've got a lot of nerve." Mrs. Peterson scowled at me, refusing to sit.

"You guys have it all wrong." I snatched up the *Weekly Wine*. "I am *not* dating Colin Hillson. I'm not dating anyone."

"Oh, we know, honey," Mrs. Chapman said. "That, we could handle, but this is the most disappointing thing anyone in this town has ever done. How could you?"

"How could I what? I have no idea why everyone is mad at me. So, whatever you three are babbling about, out with it." I crossed my arms over my chest, glaring at the women responsible for spreading whatever ridiculous thing they thought I'd done to the whole town.

"We found out the truth. How could you even think about taking Orchard Hill Farms to *Hidden Cove* of all places? It's a betrayal." Mrs. Jeffries had tears in her eyes.

"Oh, that." My shoulders fell. They really did hate me, and I couldn't face Mrs. Jeffries and her tears.

"Yes, that." Mrs. Chapman glowered over me, and I felt nine years old again. "Honey, what were you thinking?"

"Well, you can blame Conner Ashford for everything." I stood to leave, clutching my library books to my chest. "If I'm going to keep Orchard Hill afloat for the next generation, then I have to expand. To do that, I need land, and the Ashfords control everything in this town." I was dangerously close to tears, and I had to get out of here before I completely lost it in front of these women. The whole town would hear about it before dinner time.

"That stupid feud again?" Mrs. Peterson rolled her eyes. "Do you Contrerases and Ashfords even know what started it all? The whole town is sick of it."

"It's idiotic, but I have to do what's right for my family and the business we've spent generations cultivating. If I can't do that here in Superiore Bay, then I have to take my business elsewhere. It's nothing personal." I shoved past three of the sweetest ladies I'd ever known and headed across the square to find Enzo. I had to get out of here.

Chapter Nineteen

CONNER

Selena Contreras, Sleeping With the Enemy

I couldn't seem to stop myself from looking at that stupid picture of Selena with Colin Hillson. He was such a loser. And he was too young for Selena. Not that she couldn't date whoever she wanted. What did I care?

She could do so much better than a Hillson. Especially that Hillson. Colin liked to think he and his family were better than the Ashfords, but they were copycats. Everything the Ashfords did for Superiore Bay, they did for Hidden Cove. If we made a donation to a local charity or to the high school, they just had to one up us and give a bigger donation to a Hidden Cove charity or school. It was embarrassing. For them.

"What does she see in this guy?" I tried to turn my focus back to approving the inventory reports, but I couldn't keep my mind on the boring task. I'd gone into the main offices this morning, but I was so distracted, I came here where no one could see me struggling.

Duke nudged my knee, trying to shove his way under my desk. He liked to hide under there and lay on my feet. "I'm moving, I'm moving." I slid back to give him room to settle in the bed I kept under there for him.

This time, Duke laid his head on my knee, giving me sad I'm-sorry-you're-so-pathetic eyes.

"I'm not pathetic." I scratched between his ears, and I swear his look said, 'Yes, you are, but I still love you.'

"Screw this, buddy, let's go for a drive." I knew better than to say those words before moving to a safe distance. Duke exploded from his spot under my desk and danced in circles until I extricated myself from my chair, which was now across the office.

"Easy, boy." I chuckled at his exuberance. There was nothing Duke liked better than going for a ride into town. I double checked my worn jeans and faded button down to make sure I was presentable. I tended to dress more casually whenever I knew I would spend an entire day chained to my desk. I pulled a freshly dry-cleaned shirt from the bottom drawer of my desk and quickly changed.

"All right, boy, let's go." Duke shot out of the barn and across the gravel drive to my car, waiting ever so impatiently for me to open the door. He scrambled into the backseat, and I clipped him into his seatbelt harness. I'd never forgive myself if anything happened to him if we were in an accident. It was sad, but Duke was my family and my best friend. Honestly, most days it felt like he was all I had in this world.

"Want to go visit Jake?" I grinned when Duke barked in response. My cousin Jake Ashford was probably Duke's favorite person in the world other than me. And maybe Selena Contreras. But that was only because Jake fed him cake.

I drove over the bay bridge into town, still trying to get the image of Selena with Colin Hillson out of my head. She could do so much better than that idiot.

We pulled up in front of Jake's Cakes, the best bakery in town. Duke scrambled out of the car and headed for the door.

"Let's go get coffee first." I whistled for Duke to follow me. I wasn't the most-loved person in this town, but I was used to people stopping to talk to me because they liked my dog. We walked down the street past the tea shop and the Rusty Spoon, and no one stopped us.

"Strange." I patted Duke's head and turned the corner to the Hugga Mugga. The cutesy names in this town were so awful I typically couldn't bring myself to say half of them out loud. But the tourists loved it.

"What can I get you?" The barista glowered at me.

"Large iced coffee with cream, no sugar." I smiled at the lady behind the counter, who usually talked my ear off and stuffed Duke with her homemade peanut butter dog biscuits while the barista made my coffee. For some reason, she glared back at me and ignored Duke.

That made me mad. I didn't care what people thought of me, but I drew the line at mistreating my dog, who didn't understand why he wasn't getting the A-list treatment he normally got here.

"It's okay, buddy." I scratched his head and tried not to let his crestfallen look affect me. "Could the big guy get a couple of those dog biscuits?" I plastered on my best smile.

"They're a dollar a piece." The lady refused to look at me. "Can't be giving them away for free when all you buy is iced coffee."

"No problem." I let a hard edge enter my voice. "He doesn't know the difference between free and not free, so I'll take four if you don't mind."

She nodded, looking ashamed and rightfully so.

Duke swallowed the first two whole, and I gave him a third one on the way out to Jake's Cakes. "You can have the last one tonight. We can't spoil your supper."

Duke rolled his eyes at me. He knew as well as I did, he'd eat until he exploded.

As we walked back down the street, I could have sworn everyone we passed gave me a dirty look. I glanced down at my fresh shirt, wondering if the dry cleaner didn't get it clean.

"Get out of here with that crap!" Jake yelled at me, pointing for the door before we even got inside his bakery.

"What, this delicious and refreshing iced coffee beverage from the amazing Hugga Mugga?" I grinned at my cousin, who refused to serve iced coffee of any kind in his bakery. He also had a healthy rivalry with the coffee shop—bordering on ridiculous. The two shop owners hated each other, but it provided a great source of entertainment for the rest of the town.

"No outside food or drinks." Jake pointed to the sign above the counter that expressly forbid beverages from Hugga Mugga. He was busy working on a three-tiered birthday cake with a dinosaur made of copious amounts of icing wrapped around the edge. Some kid was going to have an epic birthday cake.

I ignored him and leaned over the counter. "Duke would like a slice of your best carrot cake please. And I'll take a caramel brownie."

Jake shook his head, moving to the cake display case. "You know, just because it has carrots in it doesn't make it a healthy choice for the dog. He'd be better off with a piece of fruit."

"It's his one vice. We come here, he expects cake, and he loves carrots." Duke sat back on his haunches, resting his chin on the counter and laying his ears back with his best poor-me-I'm-so-hungry expression that literally no one could resist.

"Here, boy." Jake smiled, setting a plate with a small slice of carrot cake on the floor.

"Hi, Jake dear." Mrs. Abernathy from the library shuffled up to the counter. "I need two slices of your strawberry cassata cake to go. I can't go home without it or my husband will have a fit. He just loves your cakes."

"Thanks, Mrs. Abernathy." Jake moved to pack up the order, and Mrs. Abernathy turned to give me the same dirty look everyone else had given me since I drove into town. She ignored me and turned her attention on Duke, muttering something about how the poor boy couldn't help who his dad was.

"Here you are, Mrs. Abernathy." Jake set the to-go bag on the counter. "You tell Mr. Abernathy I'm working on a new recipe for a pina colada cake that's right up his alley."

"Oh, he'll just love that." She shoved a quarter into the tip jar and shot me another withering look before she shuffled out the door.

"What was that about?" I asked Jake. "You saw that, right?"

"The old lady stare down? Yeah, I saw it. You're in the dog house, cuz."

"But why? What don't I know?"

Just then, my phone rang, and I didn't recognize the number. "Conner Ashford," I answered in my professional voice, never knowing when the call would be work related.

"Mr. Ashford, I'm a representative of the city council of Superiore Bay. We are calling to request the presence of an Ashford family representative—specifically you—at five PM this evening at the Superiore Bay Historical Society and Museum."

"Come again?" I scowled at the absurdity of this call. Why would the town council want to meet me at the historical society and not the town hall?

"Be at the historical society at five PM tonight." The line went dead.

"She hung up on me." I stared down at the phone.

"Who?" Jake wiped down his counter and shoved the bag with my brownie across the perfectly clean surface.

"Some weird lady from the city council. They want me to attend a meeting at five."

"Well, you better get over there; it's almost five now, and you do not want the town council coming after you. They take their job seriously."

"Come on, Duke, looks like we have a meeting to get to." The Historical Society was down the street and around the corner from Jake's Cakes. We walked into the old musty museum just after five PM. I heard raised voices, lots of them. And I also heard my name several times before I stepped into the small auditorium where they normally showed old documentaries about the town history. Now, I knew why they wanted to meet here. It seemed like every business owner in Superiore Bay was here, and they were angry.

"There he is." Mrs. Patterson pointed at me, and I felt the sudden urge to run before they came at me with pitchforks and torches.

"What do you have to say for yourself, young man?" A woman I didn't even know stood with her hands on her hips, looking for all the world like she might ground me and send me to bed without my supper.

A hundred voices echoed her demand, and I reached to give Duke a calming pat on the head before he started growling. "I think we're in trouble, boy." I started to take a step back, but someone closed the doors behind me.

Chapter Twenty

LENA

I wasn't sure what exactly was going on.

Half an hour ago, I received a call to get to the historical society as soon as I could. The lady on the phone had practically yelled at me. I'd just gotten home, but Enzo drove me back here in his truck. When I walked in, it had looked like the entire town was waiting for me.

The entire angry town.

They looked a bit more sympathetic toward me than they had earlier in the day, but there was still an undercurrent of angst. And suddenly, I knew what this was about.

What followed was twenty minutes of the town trying to convince me to tell them what the Hillsons were offering me to open my new business venture in Hidden Cove. The town council claimed they could match anything their rivals gave me. But I knew that wasn't true.

I stood up to quiet the rabble, and voices faded to a soft murmur. "I'm sorry you all had to find out this way, and I know you feel betrayed, but I'm afraid I don't have a choice. Hidden Cove isn't only offering tax breaks and incentives. If they were, I'd have come here to give Superiore Bay the same chance. The Hillsons are willing to become silent partners, investing in my plans. I can't pass up an opportunity like that."

Trevor Ashford, Conner and Carter's youngest uncle, who was known to be on the outs with his family, stood to face me. "Have you signed the contract yet?"

I shook my head. "But it's only a matter of time. I must think of my family."

"What about the town?" I didn't see who spoke next.

My eyes searched the crowd, taking in the familiar faces. "I love this town. You all know I do. It's in my blood. I grew up here, my family has lived here for generations. We helped build Superiore Bay, but we can't always let rivalries derail our futures."

"Is that the only rivalry you're willing to let go of?" It was Carter, the same Carter who hadn't been answering my calls. "Superiore Bay and Hidden Cove?"

"For now, it's the one offering me a truce."

Carter stood. "Maybe whoever took that picture did you a favor."

How could he say that? Whoever took that picture caused this entire mess. To my surprise, Enzo, sitting next to Carter for some strange reason I couldn't fathom, nodded along with his words. Something was definitely up with the two of them.

There was no way I was going to get through to this crowd. With a weary sigh, I sat, and the rumbling cranked up again.

Sierra Gonzalez, the head of the council, tried to regain control, but even she failed. It wasn't until the door at the back of the room opened everyone quieted. Conner walked through, stopping in his tracks as he took in the meeting.

He looked blindsided, just as I had. Had Sierra called him too?

I tried to say something with my eyes, but he turned away, looking like he might try to escape out the door again. Only,

Jake Ashford walked in, shutting the doors and cutting off any hope Conner had of getting out of this.

Conner turned on his heel, his confidence never wavering as he walked farther into the room with every eye on him. "What's going on?"

Sierra pulled a folding chair to the front and pointed to it. "Conner Ashford, sit down."

His steps slowed. "Am I on trial?"

She didn't smile at his attempted joke. "Yes."

"Off with his head," someone yelled. I looked around, finding Max Ashford, sitting next to his father, a smile stretching his young face.

A few people snickered at that. Conner shot his cousin a glare.

I settled my eyes on Carter and Enzo, who were both grinning as they whispered to each other. My eyes narrowed before turning back to Conner.

Sierra circled his chair, her long arms crossed over her chest. Dark curls settled around her shoulders. She was young for a councilwoman, much less someone who led the council. Only Harrison Ashford held more power in this town as the mayor.

"Did I miss the show?" My grandmother slid into the empty chair next to me.

"What's going on, Gram?"

She only shrugged, a sneaky grin on her face.

I thought back over this entire awful day. The stares. The harsh words. Everything that was now directed at Conner. I sucked in a breath when I realized what was happening. In my anger, I'd revealed Conner was the reason I had to look elsewhere for my business. It wasn't even really his fault, more like his father's, but he'd be blamed for it.

Covering my face with my hands, I let out a body-rattling sigh. A presence bumped legs as he pushed his way down the aisle to my right. I lowered my hands to find Duke staring at me. "Hey, boy," I whispered. "I think I got your dad in trouble."

"Conner Ashford," Sierra started. "What do you have to say for yourself?"

"Um …" Confusion clouded his voice. "I don't know."

She scoffed. "You don't know? Okay, I'll ask you some questions."

"Whatever you feel the need to do."

"What town do we live in?"

His brow furrowed. "Superiore Bay."

She nodded. "And what town do we want to see grow and expand? What town would we like to see allow its business owners to thrive?"

"Superiore Bay," someone yelled.

Sierra pointed to them. "Exactly. We can't do that when two of our most prominent families are feuding."

"This can't be happening," I muttered.

Gram patted my knee. "Everything will work out the way it's meant to, *Mija*."

I wasn't sure what she meant by that exactly, but she threw a look at Carter and Enzo over her shoulder that stirred my suspicion.

Duke rested his head in my lap, and I curled my fingers into his fur, drawing strength from him before shooting to my feet. "Stop this please."

Sierra cast me a withering look. "This is none of your concern, Lena."

"Of course it is. It's completely my concern."

"No," someone else yelled. "It's the town's concern."

I turned to face the crowd. "This is why you've all come here today? To bully one of your own?" Duke let out a low growl as if he agreed that this was ridiculous.

Sierra eyed the dog warily.

Someone pushed himself off the back wall and strode

forward. When he got closer, I recognized Harrison Ashford. The crowd that was two seconds from becoming a mob quieted in the presence of the popular mayor.

Harrison stopped near Conner, looking down at him. He didn't turn to us as he said, "Lena is right." Finally, he looked back. "But so are we." His eyes settled on me. "Lena, I hope you understand it's only fear behind all of this. We believe in what you're trying to do and think it will be a great success in driving tourism. We cannot allow you to give that advantage to Hidden Cove or the Hillson family."

Conner's eyes met mine, as if finally realizing what my meeting in that diner was actually about. I could have been wrong, but I thought I saw guilt in his eyes. For the first time, he realized this was all his family's fault.

"Force them to give her the land," Barrett Ashford, Conner's older uncle said. "It's time the Ashford-Contreras feud ended."

If only it were that easy. My parents weren't here, and neither was Conner's father. We couldn't put an end to anything while they continued to hate each other.

I shook my head. "Even if they sold me the land, I still don't have the capital I need. The Hillsons offered me a way that doesn't involve me putting my family's entire legacy at stake." I glanced at Enzo. "I won't risk our future."

Harrison pursed his lips, looking from Conner to me. "You said nothing is official with Colin Hillson, correct?"

I nodded. Nothing had been signed yet.

I ignored the rest of the crowd, zeroing in on Harrison, who was obviously deep in thought. I was sure I wouldn't like whatever he was considering.

Harrison nodded, as if he'd come to a conclusion. "There's only one way to solve this."

I wasn't the only one hanging on his every word. Conner stared at him like his gaze could burn holes right through his cousin.

I could almost guess the words that were about to come from his lips. His satisfied smile said it all.

"Conner will invest."

A round of laughter, coming mostly from Ashfords, wound through the crowd. Max, Emery, their older brother, Grant. Harrison's siblings. Both of Conner's uncles. The only family member present not laughing was Carter. Instead, he looked way too pleased with himself.

Harrison waited for his family to stop laughing. "I wasn't joking. This is the only solution. Selena needs an investor. Conner has money to invest and not enough sense to offer it himself. Tying the families together will put a lid on this impossible feud." His stern gaze met mine. "And better yet, this is what's good for the town."

I caught the meaning behind his words as my stomach sank to the bottom of the bay. If I said no, I was putting myself over the town, and that wasn't done in Superiore Bay. Bile rose in my throat at the thought of working with Conner, of letting him have a piece of what I'd been dreaming of for years.

Did achieving my goal have to mean giving up a part of my pride?

And was it worth it?

The answer to the second question was easy. Yes. Pride had no place in business, in dreams. It would only hold me back.

I didn't hear what was said after, and only minutes later, the crowd dispersed, leaving me staring at Conner with Duke between us.

I wasn't sure how this had just happened, but I hoped it didn't ruin everything.

Neither of us moved. I barely breathed as our eyes connected and we both realized there was no getting out of this. Not in this town.

Chapter Twenty-One

CONNER

What was I supposed to do now?

Lena ran out of the meeting last night before talking to me. She just stared and left, as if this was all my fault. Couldn't she see I didn't want this any more than she did?

Except now, I couldn't get it out of my head.

What had Colin Hillson so interested? As far as I knew, Lena just wanted to open up a store. What was so special about that? Why did Hidden Cove want this so badly?

I had to find out.

I stared at my desk, realizing how much work I had to do today. One of our suppliers received an off batch of wine, and I needed to figure out why, but heading over to the winery held no appeal.

I was standing over my desk when my grandfather walked in, curiosity in his gaze. "I just got an interesting phone call."

"Yeah? I'd love to hear about it when I get back." I patted my leg, calling Duke to my side.

My grandfather stopped me at the door. "It was from Valentina Contreras."

That made me pause. "What is Valentina Contreras doing calling you?" I'd never heard him mention Lena's grandmother.

He waved my question away. "Oh, us old coots have no use for family squabbles. We witnessed enough squabbling when we were young."

"Okay, so what did she say?"

"Apparently I missed an impromptu town meeting last night."

I groaned. "Don't remind me."

"Does your father know about this new arrangement?"

I shrugged, trying to act like I didn't care. In reality, that was the reason I barely slept the night before. He wasn't going to be happy, and I'd never been the son to cross him. That honor went to Conrad and Carter. Not to mention both of my father's brothers, who wanted little to do with the winery.

Sometimes, I wondered if I cared too much for a man who didn't care about me, but I was all he had other than his own father, and I couldn't leave him on his own. Plus, I loved the winery and every acre of vineyard. It was home.

With a sigh, I stopped in the hallway. "I don't want to tell him until I know what this town-forced partnership will entail." I already knew I wouldn't use Ashford money. That would come with too many strings, and not even Lena Contreras deserved that.

No, this had to come from the trust fund my mother left me, the money my father couldn't touch.

I left my grandfather, who looked way too contemplative. I didn't want to know what he and Valentina Contreras were conspiring about. What I did want to know was how this would work.

And only one person could tell me that.

I drove toward Orchard Hill, passing under a rusty archway

depicting the name of the farm surrounded by apples. The dirt road kicked up dust under my tires. I would need to get my car washed after coming out here. I always did.

The Contreras family home came into view, a modest Victorian style home that had seen better days. Across the yard was the barn where I found Duke the last time I was here, and a small bunkhouse Lena shared with her brother.

Duke had been upset, but this time, I left him at home.

The orchard stretched along the horizon, an orchard I now had an interest in. If I was going to invest in this business venture, we'd do it right. There was no chance of failure. Ashfords didn't fail.

I stepped out of the car, but there was no one around. Swallowing my pride, I knocked on the front door. Footsteps sounded on the other side, and when Lena's mother opened the door, my heart sank. I'd hoped it would be her grandmother. At least she didn't glare at me.

"What can I do for you?" Luciana Contreras wiped her hands on the apron tied around her waist. I wanted to know if she'd heard about the meeting, but I couldn't find the words. She was an intimidating woman with her hard, dark eyes, hair pulled back tightly, and a mother's protectiveness over her kids. She reminded me of my own mother.

I cleared my throat. "I'm looking for Selena."

She rolled her eyes to the ceiling, muttering something in Spanish I didn't understand, but I did catch the word *idiota*, and it wasn't hard to figure out what that meant. "She isn't here." She tried to swing the door shut, but I caught it with my hand.

"Please, I need to speak with her."

"I can't keep that girl away from you Ashfords, can I? *Dame paciencia, señor.*" She slid the door open wider. "I might regret this, but Selena will come in for lunch soon. You can wait."

I wasn't sure that was such a good idea, but I followed her

inside anyway. She led me through their modest living room, past a worn leather sectional, and into a bright kitchen. Big windows spanned the wall above the sink, letting the sunlight stream across smooth granite countertops and aged wooden floors. Jars were stacked across the counter along with baskets of apples and bowls of what looked like jam.

Mrs. Contreras shoved things around on the counter before stirring whatever it was she had in a pot on the stove.

I didn't get to ask about it before the door burst open. "Luci." Mr. Contreras walked in, not noticing me as he kissed his wife on the cheek. "I'm going to clean up before lunch."

A few others came in behind him I didn't recognize. I assumed they worked at the orchard. Each gave me a nod before heading to the sink to wash their hands.

Next, was Enzo. He stopped when he saw me, a slow smile creeping over his face. "Here to obey the town?"

I looked to make sure his mother hadn't heard. "Something like that."

He clapped a hand on my shoulder, a far cry from the indifference he'd once had for me.

The door opened one final time, and in walked Lena, dirt smeared across her face. She didn't wear overalls today, but her jeans were filthy, and her light green t-shirt wasn't faring any better. Two messy braids hung over her shoulders. Even when she was a mess, there was something intriguing about her, something that prevented me from looking away.

When she noticed my presence, the color drained from her face. "What are you doing here?" The rest of the people in the kitchen ignored our stand-off.

"We need to talk."

"We absolutely do not." She walked away from me, sidling up to her mom.

"*Mami*, what's for lunch?"

"Patience, *Mija*. That's what you're having. Shoo, the sauce is almost ready." She lowered her voice, but I could still hear her. "Go find out what that man wants so you can get him out of here."

I sighed. This was going to be harder than I thought.

Lena walked back toward me, her shoulders dipping in resignation. "Outside." She walked out the swinging screen door, letting it slam behind her.

When I reached her, she whirled to face me. "Let's get one thing straight, Ashford. I don't need you."

"I know."

"I ... what?"

I ran a hand through my hair. "Look, Lena, I know you can do this without me, that it's probably more appealing to take Colin Hillson on as a partner. But I can promise you, nothing in your life will be easy if you do that."

"Is that a threat?" She stepped toward me.

"What? No, of course not. But this town, they'll never forgive you."

She sighed, and I could tell she knew it too. This was her only option. "If you'd have just sold me the land to begin with ..."

"And the money? Did you have it?" I knew for a fact the bank had turned down her loan. She didn't answer, so I kept going, "I know you think I'm this horrible person, and I'm going to have to go over your plans to see if I have any hope of recouping my investment, but the town seems to think we need this, so we at least have to try."

Those were the wrong words. Her gaze hardened. "I don't have to do anything. Do you know how long I've dreamed of this, Conner? How many hours I've spent with Eli, going over every little legal issue? And now, you want to come in and be my white knight, throwing your money around. Before you even know if you believe in me."

That wasn't what I'd said, right? It wasn't her I needed to verify, only the business. I wanted to tell her I knew she could do anything, but the words stuck in my throat. I ended up staring at her like the fool her mother said I was. *Idiota.* Yep.

She didn't seem to notice my loss for words as she crossed her arms. "I won't let the Ashfords take everything I have."

The more she argued, the more I wanted to be part of this, the more I had to. It was like she'd issued the ultimate challenge. I didn't want to take anything of hers, but I couldn't let it go.

Irritation rose in me, not a new sensation around her. I inched closer until I stared directly into her eyes. Dipping my head, I brought our faces close. "There's no way out of this, Lena." Her breath hitched, and I could feel its irregular rhythm. I needed to step back, right now, but I couldn't. Something held me in place.

"There's always a way out," she whispered.

I gave my head the tiniest shake. "Not this time. The town won't have it."

We stayed that way for a long time. Too long, until a throat clearing behind us made me jump back to a safe distance.

Enzo leaned against the back porch, a smirk on his lips.

With a growl, Lena stormed past him, muttering, "Don't eavesdrop," as she entered the house.

I wasn't sure what had just happened, but I had to get out of here.

I turned toward my car, but Enzo's voice made me stop. "Don't leave yet. Wait there."

Something in his tone made me listen to him. So, I waited in my car, knowing Lena and her parents were probably staring at me through the windows. When Enzo came jogging back out, I rolled down my window. He handed me a folder.

"What's this?"

"Just look through it." He walked back into the house.

When I got home, I didn't go back to work. Instead, I asked my grandfather to go to the winery to figure out what went wrong with the bad batch. He was pleased to be given any responsibility when my father no longer let him be involved.

I took a long shower, washing off the morning. Whatever Mrs. Contreras had been cooking for lunch had smelled amazing, and it had made me hungry. I dried off and threw on a pair of jeans, not bothering with a shirt as I made my way to the kitchen. Our cook had left some kind of fish in the fridge for lunch, but what I really wanted was whatever that barbecue scent had been.

Barbecue was comfort food, and we didn't get much of that around here. With a sigh, I grabbed a hard-boiled egg out of the fridge and cut up some cheese. It was basic, but it was the only appetizing thing I could find.

I returned to my room and stared at the accusing folder Enzo had given me. My gut told me Lena didn't know I had it. But I was too curious not to look inside.

Flipping open the cover, I popped a piece of cheese into my mouth and started reading. It was her business plan, complete with profit projections, graphs, and even a list of everything she hoped to accomplish.

There were sketches of what the buildings would look like —more than one of them. It was more like a complex of buildings, a destination, each with a different purpose. She'd designed everything to be more than a simple expansion of her family's business. A trip here would be an experience.

My lunch forgotten, I spent the next hour going over everything, only finding small issues, but nothing that made me think it was a bad investment. This business ... it wouldn't only help the Contreras family. The entire town would benefit.

No wonder they'd rather force us into a partnership than lose this opportunity.

My irritation toward the town faded. Because they were right. This needed to stay right here.

And I had to help make that happen.

Lena Contreras and I needed to have another chat. And this time, I wasn't letting her say no to this partnership so easily. This was her dream, and I knew in my gut that I had to be there when she achieved it.

Chapter Twenty-Two
LENA

I lay awake, staring at the ceiling, the steady ticking of the hall clock grating on my nerves. I'd told Enzo a thousand times I was going to run that thing through the wood chipper, but he insisted he found it soothing.

I rolled over, praying for sleep. The first thing I was going to do in the morning was get rid of that clock once and for all. I gazed out my bedroom window at the moon rising high in the clear sky. It was different out here in the bunkhouse than in my childhood room at the big house. Much quieter.

Several years ago, Enzo and I had renovated the bunkhouse into an apartment for us. We didn't need such a big bunkhouse anymore. We couldn't afford to pay the full-time workers who would have lived here. We kept a few beds on the other end of the bunkhouse. Wishful thinking for a return of the glory days when Orchard Hill Farm was a thriving business. Not that I remembered what that was like.

My brother was still up at the house, and I had gone to bed early, hoping to lose myself in the pages of a novel. I needed to forget about the insanity of that town meeting, but even books couldn't save me now.

"How did I let this happen?" I asked the moon, but she didn't have the answers either. There had to be a way out of this forced partnership with the one man I couldn't work with. The town had picked the wrong Ashford. I could have worked with Carter as a silent investor. Even Conrad would have been a better choice.

"Conner." I said his name like a curse. He'd already shown his doubt in my plans, and he hadn't even seen them yet. I lay there envisioning how he would change everything, using his money as a means to get what he wanted. In time, he would control Orchard Hill, and my family would suffer the consequences of my dreams that had led to this disaster.

"That's what you get for dreaming too big, Lena," I whispered into the night, willing myself not to cry. I wouldn't shed a single tear over Conner Ashford.

Headlights flooded my room, and the sound of a slamming car door had me sitting up in bed. Who would come here so late at night? I looked at my phone charging on my bedside table. It was barely ten PM on a Friday night. When did I get to be such a boring person?

Someone banged on the door, the sound echoing through the sparsely furnished bunkhouse. I slipped out of bed, peeking into the hall to see if Enzo had come home yet. The apartment was tiny. Two small bedrooms, a single bathroom we shared, and a narrow hallway that led to a small living room and kitchenette. No one else was home, so it looked like I was answering the door in my pajamas.

I shivered as I walked down the hall in my shorts and t-shirt, the socks on my feet barely keeping the cool evening temperatures at bay.

"Who is it?" I hissed, hugging my arms to my chest.

"Conner."

A surge of anger warmed me up in an instant.

"What do you want?"

"Open the door, Selena, we need to talk."

I snatched the door open, fire smoldering in my belly. I was not in the mood to argue with this rich jerk tonight. "What?" I snapped.

He was holding a folder, leaning against the doorframe in his loose jeans and faded t-shirt. His hair was a mess. I looked for Duke, but he wasn't with him. This was the most un-put-together I'd ever seen Conner Ashford.

Without returning my chipper greeting, he shoved past me.

"Sure, come on in." I closed the door. "Don't wait for an invitation. But of course, you're an Ashford, so you just take whatever you want." I rolled my eyes.

"That's the first thing that has to change." He glared at me.

"Here we go." I stalked to the kitchen, shoving the tea kettle onto the hot plate. I was going to need the mother of all calming herbal teas if we were doing this tonight.

"Can we call a truce, Selena? Our first one apparently isn't in affect anymore. Neither of us want this, but we can't get out of it now, so we have to agree to be civil from this point forward. For real, this time." Conner stood with his hands on his hips, tapping his foot on my cheap linoleum floor. "Can we do that?"

"That depends." I pulled down two mugs from the wooden pegs Enzo had hung on the wall over the sink. "How much of a silent partner will you be?"

"It's a solid investment." Conner tossed his folder onto the pub table that divided the kitchenette from the living room.

"What's that?" I nodded at the folder and scooped a few teaspoons of my gram's apple chamomile and lavender tea blend—one of many I hoped to sell in our general store if we could ever get this project off the ground.

"Your brother gave it to me when I was here last. It's your business plan."

"He is dead to me." I flipped open the folder. It was everything I'd spent the last years working to develop.

"If we're going to do this, then we have to be on the same page. I have a lot of experience I can bring to the table, Selena. I can help you make this happen, but we have to work together." Conner sank into the pub chair with a sigh.

"Tea?" I lifted the kettle and poured boiling water into my mug.

"Sure." Conner nodded absently.

I brought our mugs to the table and sat down opposite him. He'd called my plans a solid investment. As much as I hated the idea of working with him, I'd at least hear him out.

"So, what are your thoughts?" I pulled the folder to the center of the table, laying out the basic building plans for each phase of the project. Without asking, I loaded both mugs with plenty of wildflower honey. It brought out the flavor of the apples in the tea.

"You're absolutely right about the location. It has to be the land parcel you wanted to buy. It's the perfect location near town." Conner ran a hand through his hair. "Honestly, it's a brilliant use of the land."

I tried to hide my smile, taking a sip of the scalding hot tea. I didn't want to get my hopes up, but I liked the passion I heard in his voice. He was into this. But that was just a quick hop and a skip away from taking over. That was one thing I would never allow.

"Let's be clear from the start, this is a silent partnership. If it's happening at all, I am in charge of this venture. You are the wallet, and that is all."

"That's not how a silent partnership works. Yes, I will provide the initial investment, but I get a say in how my investment is used. I will guide you through the project in a way that will benefit us both and allow me to recoup my investment plus a profit over time."

"See, now that just sounds like fancy business talk for taking over. Orchard Hill Farm and its future endeavors belong to me and my family."

"Selena." Conner's eyes filled with concern. "I will never take your business away from you or your family. I don't want it, and when we work with our lawyers to draft our business agreement, we will put everything in writing so you have the protection of a legal contract behind you."

The first real stirrings of hope fluttered like butterflies in my stomach. "I still don't trust you." I narrowed my eyes at him.

"It's a good idea, Selena. I want to be part of it."

"Ashford money feels like blood money." I sipped my tea, wondering how I'd gotten myself into this mess.

"Well, then, it's a good thing we won't be relying on Ashford money." Conner smiled, his eyes lighting up with mischief.

"Wait, what now?"

"My father doesn't need to be part of this, so any investment I use for Orchard Hill will come from my personal funds that my father doesn't control."

I nodded. "I like the sound of that." Hope was a scary thing when one had to put their trust in someone they despised. "We need to discuss every aspect of how this will work leading up to phase one of construction."

Conner took a sip of his tea and leaned forward, eager as I was whenever I talked about this project. "That's where I want to make the first big change. You're thinking too small, Selena. With an investor, we don't need to phase it out. Go big or go home, right?" He picked up the master drawing that showed where I wanted to be in ten years. "We go right to phase four and hit the ground running."

"Absolutely not." I stared at him, wondering how he ran a successful business. "We start with phase one." I lifted the phase one drawing that showed two small buildings closest to town.

The general store and the cider cafe. "We use phase one to pay for phase two." Phase two was the restaurant and the Christmas shop that would open seasonally for the first two years. We would sell Orchard Hill Christmas trees, and eventually, it would stay open year round.

"We will earn the highest profit margins if we go straight to phase four this year."

"This year? Are you nuts?" I gathered up all the documents and shoved them back in the folder. "That's a great way to go bankrupt within the first three years." My entire business plan was based on building up to phase four. "This whole venture is a huge risk." I shook my head. "Phase one is the best way to build slowly over time without risking losing everything."

"It's a big change, I know that." Conner sipped his tea. "Let it sink in, and we can talk about it again later."

"No. If we're going to do this, we're doing it my way."

"This tea is really good." Conner took another sip. "Really good."

"It's my gram's blend. She makes it with chamomile from her garden and our pink lady apples. The wild flower honey Mr. Peterson bottles is what makes it even better."

"That's what I'm talking about." Conner leaned forward. "This tea should be on our shelves."

"It will be, in phase three when we add the Superiore Bay market. I want a place for all the local vendors to sell their products on consignment. From Mr. Peterson's wild honey to Mallory Ellison's apple-cherry chutney, and Rusty's applewood smoked bacon, Mrs. Chapman's goat cheese, and Mr. Webber's prize-winning butternut squash. This town has so much to offer. I want them to have a place to showcase the things they're most proud of."

Conner smiled. "That is my favorite part of your plan. What an incredible way to give back to the community."

"In phase three."

"Think of it, Selena. This time next year, you could have it all up and running." He smiled over his mug.

"You're insane." I drained the last of my tea and took my mug to the sink. "It's too much too soon."

"If you didn't have an eager investor willing to fund the project, it would be way too fast. But you do have a very talented, business savvy investor who can front the money to make it happen." Conner stepped up behind me, setting his empty mug in the sink.

I turned around, daring to hope. "Show me the figures."

"Really?" He grinned.

I nodded, feeling like I could puke. "I need to see the projections and the debt ratios. If I'm doing this, I want to be in the black within five years."

"That's doable."

I couldn't help the smile that spread across my face. "Are we doing this?"

Conner grabbed me and pulled me into his arms. "Yes, we're doing it! You won't regret it, Selena, I promise." And then, the *idiota* kissed me. His lips pressed against mine, warm and inviting. His arms held me pressed close against his chest. And I kissed him back. It had been so long since I'd been kissed, I completely lost my sanity for a single moment.

"No." I pulled back, shaking my head. "No, no, no. This," I pointed between us, "this is just business, nothing else."

"Of course." Conner's eyes filled with horror. "I got swept away in the excitement." He stepped back, putting some distance between us. "I should go." He fumbled for the door. "We'll talk again soon." He slammed the door behind him, and I leaned against it.

Oh man, that was a good kiss.

Chapter Twenty-Three

LENA

I woke up smiling for the first time in what felt like forever. Had last night really happened? Rolling onto my side, I stared out my window at the main house where I knew my parents were preparing for another day of work. They'd be horrified if they knew everything I'd agreed to.

I'd resisted partnering with Conner, but he was so excited about this, so ready to move forward, I couldn't help feeling the same things. Phase four. He wanted to move straight to phase four.

The Conner Ashford I thought I knew was cautious, the stern and hard businessman who did what Daddy told him. But maybe I hadn't really known him at all. Last night, he hadn't been hard or cautious. There'd been an almost childlike glee in his eyes when he talked about the business. Almost like he needed this just as much as I did.

And then, that kiss …

I squeezed my eyes shut, needing to forget that moment or the fact I wanted to go back and not let it end.

My phone chirped from my bedside table, and I pulled it free of the charger. Carter. Guilt gnawed at me. What would he say if he knew I kissed his brother? If he knew how much I'd enjoyed it.

But business and … non-business stuff couldn't mix. I had too much riding on this.

With a sigh, I answered the phone. "Why are you up so early?" It was six in the morning, not an unusual time for me to get the day started, but Carter was pretty much the opposite.

"I do that sometimes," was his reply.

I snorted. "You do not, but okay."

"What are you doing today?"

I rolled onto my back and stared at the whirring fan blades overhead. "Working. What else?" I was always working.

"Play hooky with me today."

"Can't."

"You can, you just won't."

I laughed at that. "True, but some of us have jobs, Carter. I thought your father was going to make you start working for the family."

"He hasn't decided where to put me in the empire so I can't screw anything up."

Despite my joking, I felt bad for Carter. He'd never known exactly what he wanted to do with his life, only that he didn't want it to have anything to do with wine. He had a trust fund that meant he'd survive if he never got a job his entire life, but no one wanted to be so aimless.

"Well, you could always come out to the orchard for some manual labor."

"Lena? Are you there?" Crackling came over the line but, despite our bad reception, I knew what he was doing. I rolled my eyes. "Lena?"

"Oh no, Carter. Guess reception is cutting out." My voice was monotone, but I doubted he noticed.

"That's a shame. Crackle crackle. Wanted. Crackle. To help you." And the line went dead.

My best friend was ridiculous, but I loved him for it.

Yelling came from the main house, and I jumped out of bed, pulling on my bathrobe, before hustling outside and across to the kitchen door. My parents stood facing each other in the kitchen, my dad's face so red I was afraid he'd explode.

Gram stood near the door, and when she saw me, she shook her head in warning, but I needed to know what was going on. Neither of my parents saw me enter.

"She's my daughter!" my father yelled. "I have every right to be upset." He and Mom started speaking so rapidly in Spanish I couldn't keep up. I spoke the language, but not nearly as frequently or as well as them.

I caught small snippets of conversation. My mother had seen Conner's car here last night, but she didn't seem to know who it was, only that I had a late visitor.

Dad was angry she hadn't woken him so he could confront whoever it was.

My eyes widened as I realized what they thought happened. My parents thought I had a man spend the night, that he'd left early this morning. Embarrassment flooded me and a flush rose in my cheeks.

"Stop!" I yelled. This was what I got for being secretive.

Both my parents looked at me in shock. "*Mija*," Mom started.

Dad took a step toward me. "Lena, I know you're an adult, but you are also living on my property. Unmarried young people should see each other at appropriate hours."

"Please stop." I couldn't take this much longer. "My ears are bleeding." I looked to my grandmother for help, but she seemed to be having trouble suppressing a laugh. The traitor.

I sucked in a breath. "It was Conner Ashford."

Both my parents exploded in chatter again, but I hardly caught any of it as they talked over each other. I probably should have led with the why instead of the who.

"Quiet!" I crossed my arms.

Both went silent until Mom put an arm around my shoulders. "*Mija*, the Ashfords are not the kind of company we wish you to keep."

"Why?"

"What?"

"Gram told me the history of our two families. Keeping that past alive is stupid."

"Lena." My father leveled me with a stern stare. "Watch how you speak."

I groaned. "Come on. This entire town is sick and tired of the feud you two and Mr. Ashford insist on continuing. The rift happened generations ago, and you still act like we're the Capulets and Montagues. We're not. Not even close. Do you know why?"

"We aren't killing each other?" Enzo's voice came from the doorway.

"No." I stared at each member of my family in turn. "They weren't in danger of losing everything."

No one responded, and I swear we could have heard a drop of sweat hit the wooden floor.

Mom covered her mouth with her hand. Dad's brows drew together in frustration. Enzo stared at his feet.

But Gram, I could've sworn there was pride in her gaze.

Finally, Dad met my gaze. "Lena, we aren't in danger—"

"Don't say it." I shook my head. "Grandfather left me his shares. Me. I never knew why he didn't leave them to you or to Enzo, not until recently. He knew the struggles we faced, the struggles we'd continue to face. Orchard Hill Farm hasn't seen a high profit year in half a decade. I've been over the books. We're leveraged up to our ears, which isn't a problem right now, but one day, it will be. If we don't make a change, if we don't do something to draw visitors and distributors, there won't be a family business left for me and Enzo."

Mom drew in a deep breath. This wasn't new information to them, but none of us had been so blunt, so honest about it before. "I don't understand what this has to do with Conner Ashford spending the night."

"He didn't spend the night." I looked at my brother. It was time. "Will you go out to the bunkhouse? There's a folder on the pub table. Please bring it here."

He nodded and slipped outside.

I felt pressure in my hand and caught Gram's smile out of the corner of my eye.

"You might want to sit down." I gestured to the small kitchen table where Mom's jam making supplies were piled up. She always had some project working in the kitchen, but making jam and jarring it always took the longest.

Enzo returned a moment later with my folder. I opened it and set it on the table to start pulling out papers, starting with the drawings.

"There are four planned phases." I laid the pictures in order. "Originally, my plan was to do them one at a time to avoid taking on too much risk."

My father only gave the pictures a quick glance before looking at me. "I thought we gave up on this outlandish idea. We cannot begin a new business just because one is failing."

"No, *Papi*. You gave up on it. I never did." I pulled out the business plan. "Our current struggles are precisely the reason we should do this now. Everything about this opportunity connects to Orchard Hill. It will bring tourists up the coast to our small town, tourists who will spend money in the local economy. I want to provide opportunities for this town, for these people. For us."

I slid onto the chair next to him. "No one gets anywhere playing it safe." Reaching for the drawing of phase four, I handed it to him. "This is my dream."

No one spoke for a long moment until my mother asked, "What does Conner Ashford have to do with your dream?"

This was where things got tricky. I rubbed the back of my neck. "If you two came to town meetings, you'd have seen the entire town push us together. They don't want us working against each other. I needed an investor."

Darkness flashed across my father's face, and he set the drawing down. "No." Without another word, he stood and walked from the room, leaving the rest of us staring after him.

"Lena." My mother sighed. "The Ashfords are not our friends. Their money will always have strings attached." Her expression softened. "You have done a wonderful job with all of this." She gestured to the papers. "And we can discuss how to move forward on a smaller scale, but we will not take anything from that family."

She followed my father, leaving Gram and Enzo to stare at me with sympathy.

Gram took a seat beside me. "You're right about your grandfather. He knew you'd take the risks necessary to lead this family in the right direction."

"But is it the right risk?" Maybe my parents had a point. Conner might seem easy to work with now, but how long could that last? I thought back on that kiss, wondering if that too had been a part of the business discussions, a way to make sure I agreed.

Enzo sank into a chair with a huff and shuffled through the papers until he found what he was looking for. He pointed to phase one. "Who dreamed this up?"

"Me?"

"Was that a question?"

I shrugged.

"Lena." His gaze met mine. "This entire idea was yours. Not our parents'. Not mine or Gram's. No one dreamed of this except you. Can you really let them make you doubt yourself?"

"But what if they're right? What if I'm making a giant mistake?"

Enzo let out a dramatic sigh. "Okay, I'm going to tell you something, and you have to promise not to get mad."

I rolled my eyes. "Fine."

"Carter took that picture of you and Colin Hillson."

I shot to my feet, and my chair fell over behind me. "What? Enzo, I had one of the worst days because of that photo. This town hated me."

Enzo had the decency to at least look ashamed. "As soon as you said you were going to expand your land search to Hidden Cove, we knew we had to do something."

"We?" All the whispering and secret meetings.

"We planted that story in the *Weekly Wine* and then spread the rumor about you looking to open a business outside of Superiore Bay."

I crossed my arms over my chest and stared down at my brother, wishing my gaze could burn holes right through his head. "And why did you think it was a good idea to make me a pariah?"

He stood to face me. "Because, Lena, Superiore Bay is in your blood. You couldn't do business in Hidden Cove."

"The Ashfords were giving me no choice."

"That's the point. We thought the town could put pressure on the Ashfords to make sure Superiore Bay didn't miss out on this opportunity. And they did."

I pinched the bridge of `my nose. It was way too early in the morning for this. "They didn't just put pressure on them, Enzo, they made Conner part of this."

"Is that such a bad thing? Carter thinks Conner needs this too. He needs something outside of his father's world, a venture that doesn't belong to his family."

"But this is *my* venture."

"One you have no hope of even beginning without funds. We were trying to help you."

"You want to help?" I walked toward the door. "The barn needs a good scrub down today. I'm going to get dressed and head into the orchard, but that sounds like a job for such a helpful brother."

I barely breathed until I reached my bedroom and shut the door. My parents were never going to get on board, but Enzo was right. I'd never admit it to him, but I couldn't do this on my own.

He was also right about something else. This dream wasn't my family's. It belonged to me and only me.

Well, and maybe now Conner Ashford.

Help us all.

Chapter Twenty-Four

CONNER

Here I was about to embark on a new business, and all I could think about was the one moment I let myself lose control. If I were honest with myself, I wanted to kiss Lena Contreras long before last night. Maybe ever since she pushed me into the bay.

And now, I couldn't get the taste of her lips off my mind.

The way she'd responded before pulling away and deciding it wasn't a good idea. She was right, of course. If we were going to be business partners, I had to keep my distance.

Even when that was the last thing I wanted to do.

I sat in my office, staring out a wide window where I could see our vineyards in the distance. Work had been piling up, but I needed a moment to think.

It wasn't long ago I was telling Carter to stay away from Lena, that our families didn't mix. And here I was, not only tying us financially, but thinking about her way too often. I knew why my brother was drawn to her, whether it was romantically or not. She was honest, down to earth, so different from the women I'd known.

She worked hard for her family, just like I did, and wanted

nothing more than to keep the family legacy going strong. It was how I felt about our wine business. I not only wanted to lead it down its current path, but I had plans of expansion, of becoming more than what we were.

If my father would let me.

Despite my responsibilities, I had little true power in the company. That had to change. My father and I did equal shares of the work. He was about the age my grandfather had been when he turned over the business to his one son who wanted to keep it going.

I had no hopes my father would do the same.

"You look deep in thought." My grandfather stood in the doorway, his weathered face showing hints of concern.

I planned on seeking him out today because of the digging I'd done about the land Lena and I wanted. A file was open on my desk with all the documentation, but I wasn't sure if it made any difference. My grandfather wasn't one to defy my father.

"Just a lot on my mind."

He walked farther into my office. "You haven't told your father yet, have you?"

I wasn't sure how this man could always read my mind. "He won't be pleased."

"That's an understatement." He dropped into a chair across from my desk and leaned back. "You need to be prepared for his anger. If you expect it, you can weather the storm."

"Is that what you've always done?"

He sighed. "The man has always had a temper. He believes his opinions are always the right ones and doesn't like to be contradicted, but he isn't a bad man, Conner."

"I know that." I rubbed my eyes. My father never laid a hand on his kids. He wasn't violent or even cruel. He'd let Conrad leave the family business without a fight, and Carter got away with anything. And Jorgie, she was his favorite. "He's stubborn." That was the truth of it. "And afraid."

I'd always known that too. My father loved my mother more than anything, and then he lost her. He knew his attitude drove his family away. His brothers rarely spoke to him. He hardly had contact with any nieces or nephews. I was his only kid who had much to do with him.

My grandfather nodded. "He thinks control is the only way to prevent losing everything else."

I leaned forward, resting my elbows on the desk. "But it only pushes us further away."

"He will either change or learn that the hard way."

"And you? What will you do?" I lifted a single document and held it out to him. It was the deed of ownership to the plot of land Lena and I needed. "It was not purchased by the Ashford corporation, but by Willard Ashford."

His hands shook as he held the paper. "I forgot I put this in my name." A smile curved his lips. "It's no secret I loved your mother like she was my own daughter. I bought this land for her as a birthday present."

"What did she need land for?"

"She wanted to open a second facility to make specialty wines, experimental wines."

"My mom—" I hadn't known that about her. She'd been like me in the barn I'd outfitted for that purpose. I tried to recall everything I remembered, but as the years had passed, my memories of her had grown hazier.

My grandfather handed me back the document. "You can have the land."

I shook my head. "I don't want it given to us. Lena is already skeptical of having one Ashford as a partner. If we're going to do this, we need to buy the land and put it in her name."

He smiled again. "Your mother would have liked her."

"There would be no reason for my mother to have known her." I frowned. "She's my business partner. I'm her investor."

He didn't look convinced. "Tell me, can she lighten even the hardest of Ashfords? That was what your grandmother did for me. Your mother did it for your father. He used to be so easy going, so light. And you, my serious grandson, does she make you smile?"

Yes, she did. I pictured her fighting with me in front of the town, pushing me into the bay. "She's maddening."

"That's the best kind of woman."

I shook off all these notions he was trying to put in my head. "We are in business together now. It doesn't matter if she makes me … light." Whatever that meant. "Besides, no matter what partnership we form, she is still a Contreras and I'm an Ashford."

"Just names, Conner." He stood. "Remember that."

When he was gone, I tried to get back to work, but I couldn't focus. Giving up, I sent a text to Lena, telling her we got the land, which was our second biggest hurdle.

Now, I had to face my first.

I stood and reached for the suit coat I'd hung over the back of the chair, sliding it on. Taking a deep breath, I walked from the office. Some days, I worked from home, others were spent in the high-rise offices of the winery, a state-of-the-art facility. When my father was in town, he worked from here too.

His office was down the hall and around the corner from mine. I nodded to a few people I passed and sent my father's assistant a smile. "He here?"

She nodded. "Just got off a conference call."

Perfect timing. A part of me had been hoping he'd be too busy to see me.

I lifted a hand, knocking forcefully three times. My father respected strength, and that even applied to how one knocked, how they shook hands.

"Come in," his gruff voice called out.

I opened the door to find him hunched over his keyboard, typing rapidly. He glanced up once before going back to what he was doing. "One moment, Conner. I need to finish this email."

I stood awkwardly, waiting for him to stop. Finally, he leaned back and met my gaze. "Do you have our third quarter profit projections ready?"

That was what I'd meant to work on all morning. "I'll have them on your desk by tomorrow."

He nodded, rubbing his chin. "What's on your mind today."

I just needed to rip off the Band-Aid, but this wasn't going to be pretty. "Can I have a seat?"

He nodded wordlessly, waiting.

"So ..." I cleared my throat.

"Conner, speak clearly and with purpose or don't waste my time."

"I'm investing in Selena Contreras' new business venture."

His brow furrowed in confusion. "Conner—"

"I know you're going to say it's a bad idea and that you refuse to let me use family money for the investment, but I have my own funds, plenty enough for this project. I believe in it, Dad. Forget who it is for a moment; we're Ashfords, do we pass up good business opportunities?"

I waited for the explosion that didn't come. Instead, he looked contemplative. "Well, no, we don't. I'm confused. I read this girl was partnering with one of the Hillson brats."

The only family my father hated more than the Contrerases. I ignored him calling Lena a *girl*. One battle at a time. "She was, but the town came together to oppose it. They asked me to invest, practically demanded. You should see her business plan, Dad. It's unbelievable. Even you would be impressed."

"You believe in this opportunity?" His expression was hard to read.

"I do. I really do. And I realized that plot of land you refused to sell her is in Grandfather's name, so even if you don't approve, we're moving forward. I want to make you proud, and I think I've done enough to do that, but making you proud isn't everything to me. Not anymore. I need to make myself proud too."

"I don't like it." Where was the anger? I was prepared for it, just like my grandfather told me to be.

"I knew you wouldn't."

"If you're going to do this, son, do it right. Silent partners don't truly have to be silent. Make sure you get a big enough share to exert your control. I don't like that family, but if they're going to succeed, it will be with an Ashford pulling the strings."

It made sense now, why he didn't blow up at me.

Control.

He wanted me to control this business venture.

I'd have laughed if I wasn't so disgusted with him, because he obviously didn't know Lena at all.

I didn't want her to work for me. I wanted to work with her, to dream her dreams and experience her triumphs.

Thoughts of her filled my head as I left my father's office. I was right to use my own funds for this, not to let him anywhere near it.

He might push businesses to great success, but he also sucked the soul right out of them.

And I refused to let that happen to Lena.

I refused to let her get hurt. By him or by me.

Chapter Twenty-Five
LENA

I stared down at the contract I was supposed to be signing. Tapping my pen on the desk, the words started running together, and my pulse pounded in my head. Should I be doing this right now? It happened so fast, my head whirled with everything Conner had thrown at me over the last few days.

"Is there something missing, Lena?" Eli flipped through his copy of the partnership agreement. "I thought we'd covered everything."

"She just needs a minute," Conner said. "We've thrown a lot at her."

How did he do that? It was like he could read my mind. "It looks great, Eli. I appreciate the way you've pulled this all together so quickly. I'm just getting nervous."

"Is there anything else we can do to make this arrangement more palatable for either of you?" Eli glanced between us.

"I can't think of a single worry that hasn't been addressed. You've really outdone yourself, protecting the interests of both my family's assets and Conner's investment." It was a dream partnership. Legally, everything would be mine within just a few years. Conner would invest his personal funds that weren't attached to the Ashford family empire, and he would recoup his initial investment plus a fair return over the course of the next five years. That was at my insistence. He wanted to give the business ten years to earn out his investment while also paying me a sizable portion of our projected profits. I insisted we make it five years, allowing for Conner to earn the bulk of the income while the business paid him back.

I wanted him out of the picture as fast as possible. If that meant I earned less than him for a few years, I was fine with that. It would still be more money than I'd ever seen. Or so Conner's projections claimed.

"Then, why aren't you signing?" Conner sounded amused.

"I'm trying." I cracked a smile, positioning the pen over the page in front of me. Anxiety gripped my chest, and I couldn't seem to make my hand move. It still felt like making a deal with the devil.

"Do you need more time to think about it, Lena?" Eli's eyes filled with concern. "We aren't pressuring you, are we?"

"Nope." I leaned over the desk. "I'm just a little terrified." I took a deep breath and signed my life away.

"Are you sure about this?" Conner asked. "A hundred percent?"

I shoved the partnership agreement across Eli's desk. "No, I'm not at all sure about this venture, but I am certain I want to do this with you. I just hope we don't lose everything."

"We won't." Conner grinned, and Duke yipped his approval. That dog really went everywhere Conner went. I wondered if he was some kind of emotional support dog because Conner wasn't himself unless Duke was with him.

I leaned back against the leather seat, exhaling a breath and feeling like a ten-thousand-pound weight had lifted off my shoulders. Whatever happened next, like it or not, we were in it together. "What now?"

Conner checked the time on his phone. "Now, we go meet

my grandfather at the bank and buy our land. Then, we'll meet with the architects."

"Oh, boy." I stood on shaky legs. "We might need to pencil in some time for my afternoon freak out."

Eli chuckled at my dry tone. "For what it's worth, Lena, this plan of yours is brilliant. I can't wait to see it come to fruition because I'm going to be your first customer."

"Thanks, Eli." Conner grinned. "We'll hold your place in line."

I felt giddy as we walked out of Eli's office and into the warm spring sunshine. "I can't believe this is finally happening." It was like my feet didn't even touch the ground as we walked down the street to the bank. My mind was floating way up in the clouds, envisioning my little village of white barn-style buildings with bright-colored flowers everywhere.

"There's Grandfather." Conner pulled me back down to earth to introduce me to yet another Ashford I had to convince. Though, Conner assured me his grandfather was more than willing to sell us the land.

"You two make a nice pair." The elderly gentleman stepped between us, offering me his arm.

"Grandfather." Conner groaned. "Behave yourself."

"I meant a pair of business partners." He ignored Conner and beamed a familiar smile at me.

"You look just like Carter."

"Trouble, with a capital T." He winked at me. I liked the grandfather immediately.

"Now, I see where he gets it."

"You know you two could just let me give you the land, and then we could all go get cake and celebrate."

"We will celebrate *after* you sell us the land, Grandfather." Conner held the door open to the Superiore Bay Bank and Trust lobby. "We are doing this all by the book."

"I meant we could go celebrate ticking off my son, but I

suppose we can celebrate your partnership too." The old man shuffled into the bank manager's office, not waiting for an invitation.

"I like him, he's feisty." I followed him.

"He's trouble." Conner shook his head. "But he's the best man I know."

"You've got the paperwork ready, Jill?" Mr. Ashford groaned as he sat in the chair in front of the bank manager's desk. "You know how I hate the paperwork."

"I'm sure you're more interested in getting to lunch than dealing with a boring old real estate sale. So, just sign away. You know the drill." Jill set a pen and stack of papers in front of Mr. Ashford, and he scribbled his signature and initials across several forms.

"This is so exciting!" Jill reached to shake my hand. "We were impressed with your business proposal back when you applied for the loan. I truly hated to deny it, but I'm glad you've found such a great investor, Lena. Your stores and restaurants will be a huge hit for tourism. And the jobs you'll bring to this town. You're an angel."

I could feel my face flush with embarrassment. I wasn't used to such high praise. "Thank you. I just hope you're right." I leaned over the forms I had to sign. I was about to make the biggest purchase of my life, and I was afraid I might lose my breakfast right on Jill's perfectly polished desk.

"I have no hesitation telling you it's going to be a huge success, and I don't hand out compliments like that very often. I can't wait to shop at your general store. Do you have any idea when it will be open?"

"We're meeting with the architects after this, and we're hoping to nail down some firm dates for breaking ground soon," Conner answered for me. That knot of anxiety was back. How was I ever going to survive moving at this rapid pace?

I was in a daze as we walked over to the architect's office.

Mr. Ashford came with us, but it was clear he was more interested in the lunch we planned to get after the meeting.

"We want to go straight to phase four," Conner announced as soon as the drawings came out. These were large scale construction documents the architects had been working on since Conner gave them the go ahead just a few days ago. Their eyes popped when they heard the news about phase four.

My anxiety vanished when I saw my dream rendered in quarter inch scale. It was happening. From the general store to the bed and breakfast inn. I saw my future flash before my eyes, and it was filled with apple-picking parties, hayrides, stables, gift shops, and a new Christmas tree farm—and one day weddings and large-scale events. My vision blurred, and I wiped furiously at my eyes. There would be time for celebratory tears and wine later. But first. Business.

"I'd still like to get the general store opened as soon as possible. I know my partner wants to get phase four underway, and I'm still trying to wrap my mind around that, but I think it's important that we have the general store open for business early next year if we can." I glanced at Conner to gauge his reaction.

"I agree with Ms. Contreras." Conner nodded, reaching over to squeeze my hand. He knew I was nervous about this and the gesture was one of reassurance, but I couldn't help but think about that kiss. "The timeline will be difficult, but I think we can get it open before the holiday season *this* year."

"Holy crap that's fast," I muttered, plastering on a smile I did not feel.

"We agree. We can handle the timeline for opening the store this year," Mark, the lead architect said. "We'd also suggest having the vast majority of the landscaping done by then as well."

"The orchard needs to happen yesterday." I tapped my finger on the space we allotted for a small apple picking orchard. "My family will transplant some of our trees from Orchard Hill Farms, but we will need to get saplings in the ground as soon as possible. It will take a few seasons for it to produce, but I plan to set up hayrides to the main orchard for the first few years anyway."

"You've thought of everything," Mark said. "I told my wife about it last night, and she wants to be the first to know when you're taking reservations at the inn. She wants at least a weekend away from the kids."

"I would say we should probably start booking in late summer for spring next year." Conner scribbled notes on his legal pad. Good thing it looked like he was going to be the organized one. I would bet just about anything he was a spreadsheet kind of guy.

"What do we do next?" I asked, feeling insecure in this office with all these guys who did these kinds of projects all the time.

Mark smiled, passing me a copy of the construction documents. "You take these home and look over everything, particularly with the landscaping plan and the general store exterior. We'll meet again in a few days to discuss any changes you want made, and I'll have some interior layout options for you to review for the general store. Then, we choose a contractor, and in a few weeks, we'll schedule dates for breaking ground, and we'll start looking at exterior finishes and landscaping materials."

"Oh my gosh." I rubbed a hand over my eyes. "This is going to be exhausting, isn't it?" I laughed, looking at Conner for confirmation.

"It's going to be epic." He grinned back at me.

Chapter Twenty-Six

CONNER

"I can't believe this is really happening." Lena grinned over her shoulder at me as she pushed open the door to the Rusty Spoon. "We're really doing this."

I couldn't help matching her smile. "I think you've said that a time or ten."

"I can't help if I'm excited."

We'd been together most of the morning, and we hadn't had a single disagreement. I let her have her silent freak outs, waiting patiently for her to realize this really was the best thing.

"Well, believe it, kids." My grandfather followed us in. "Lena, I know Conner is experienced in starting up new businesses, but you still need to get used to that top-of-the-world feeling."

I gave him a shut-up look, but he pointedly ignored me.

We found an empty table along the wall, and I took a seat, using the menu I knew by heart as a distraction.

It didn't work.

Lena cocked her head to the side, studying me. "You work

for the family business that's been in operation for generations. What new business have you started?"

"It's nothing," I muttered. I wasn't sure why I wanted to keep the fact that I made artisan wines from her. I sold them to some of our distributors, but I didn't do it for the money. It just … it felt like mine, something that didn't belong to anyone else. Probably like this business idea had felt like hers before I stepped in.

With a sigh, I lowered the menu. "Specialty wines."

She pursed her lips, and it was obvious she had no idea what I was talking about.

Luckily, I had my grandfather there to spill all my secrets. He slapped a hand on my back. "Conner grows hybrid grapes in part of the vineyard and then makes them into wines you can't get anywhere else with various flavorings and alcohol contents."

She lifted her eyes to meet mine, and I was left stunned by the depth of them. "You make wine yourself?"

One corner of my lips curled up. "You thought I was just an empty suit, didn't you?"

"Maybe." She hid her smile behind a menu.

The waitress came, and we all ordered greasy burgers, the kind I rarely ate, cheddar fries, and milkshakes. It felt like the kind of thing to get for a celebration.

When three chocolate shakes were set in front of us, I lifted mine. "A toast."

They both followed suit.

"To our new partnership."

Lena nodded. "To us."

As I sipped my milkshake, I took the chance to steal a look at her. She'd dressed up for our meetings today. In place of her overalls or dirty jeans, she wore a knee-length black skirt that showed off strong legs. Her sky blue shirt was simple, with a Vneck and cap sleeves. And her hair swept across her shoulders in soft waves.

She was beautiful.

Whether she wore overalls and braids or a skirt and makeup.

How had I never truly looked before?

"Do I have something on my face?" she asked.

"What?" I shook myself out of my trance.

"You're staring."

Both she and my grandfather were looking at me now, the latter with amusement in his eyes.

"I wasn't staring." Brilliant, Conner. Brilliant reply.

She suppressed a smile and nodded seriously. "I completely believe that."

When her eyes shifted away, I wondered if she too was thinking of the other night, of how our excitement turned into something else. Something that was probably a mistake.

The waitress returned with our food, and we all busied ourselves clogging our arteries. After a few minutes, Lena leaned in. "Do you feel like people are staring at us?"

I let my eyes scan the diner. She wasn't wrong. Mrs. Chapman and Mrs. Peterson sat in the corner, whispering to one another, their eyes on us. At the table next to them, my cousin Jake ate alone, staring at us with a furrowed brow, as if trying to figure something out. He nodded in greeting.

All around us, folks enjoying their lunch stole glances our way.

My grandfather laughed. "They're definitely staring. It isn't every day an Ashford and a Contreras breaks bread together. Even rarer yet is when they do it with smiles on their faces."

"We aren't smiling." Lena took a giant bite of her burger.

I nodded. "She's right. This is a serious business lunch. No smiling allowed." What had gotten in to me? No smiling allowed? When did I suddenly forget how to be the calm, collected Ashford? Now, all I did was make a fool of myself in front of the one woman I wanted to impress.

For business purposes, of course.

"Conner, can I ask a favor of you?" Lena suddenly didn't sound so sure of herself.

"Anything." And I meant it. I'd gone from wanting my brother to stay away from Lena to not being able to stay away from her myself.

"The news of our official partnership will get out soon, but can we try to prevent that for as long as possible?"

"Embarrassed to be working with me?"

She laughed at that. "Not anymore. But my parents … they're not okay with this. I haven't told them it's a done deal, that I made the decision. They made their feelings very clear."

How was it possible my father put up less of a fight than her parents? I could see the strain in her eyes, how she wanted her parents' approval. But it wasn't the same way I needed my father's. No, I wanted to impress him. Lena just wanted her parents' support.

I reached across the table and brushed a featherlight touch over the back of her hand. "Of course."

My grandfather's sigh made us both look at him. He rolled his eyes to the ceiling. "You know, I've always fought against this feud between the families. My father believed in it, and I'm afraid he instilled that belief in my son. Me … I wish I hadn't hidden my friendship. Maybe if we'd been open, much like you and Carter, Lena, we could have ended all of this before it infected another two generations."

"Friendship?" I asked. "With who?"

He smiled. "Valentina, of course."

"Gram?" Lena's brows shot up. "You and my grandmother were friends?"

"The best. Though, we grew apart when we both married. Then, we had children who insisted our families stay at odds.

But before all of that, when we were young, there was no closer pair."

"Like me and Carter." Lena's smile had a fondness in it that twisted something inside me.

"Exactly." He laughed. "You two always reminded me of my youth. I'd see Carter sneak off, and it brought me back. There was never anything romantic between Valentina and myself, not that anyone would've believed us. Most people don't understand how a man and a woman can be so connected to each other yet not right for each other."

"I know how that feels." Lena let out a wistful sigh. "Carter and I ... well, sometimes I think we were meant for each other. He's my soulmate. I love him like he's a part of me, but I'm not in love with him. I don't think I ever could be. It would be like falling in love with myself."

My grandfather nodded. "It's hard for anyone to fathom that kind of love who hasn't experienced it themselves."

I listened to them talk, not interjecting anything myself because they were right. It was hard to understand. I'd always thought Carter and Lena were secretly in love and just not telling anyone. Carter risked so much to be friends with her, to keep her in his life.

He chose her over his own family.

Could it be true there was nothing more than platonic love between them? Just the thought of that opened something up inside me. Hope.

It wasn't until that moment, I realized I'd been holding on to the idea of Lena and Carter as a way to ignore the feelings rising in me. Feelings I couldn't yet decipher.

Lena laughed at something my grandfather said and tucked a strand of dark hair behind her ear. Her eyes lit up as she grinned. I'd never seen her look so happy, so free.

Their conversation turned from friendship to the business we'd break ground on soon. Lena used her hands for exaggeration as she explained everything she hoped to accomplish to my grandfather. She spoke excitedly of selling local products on consignment, of attracting tourists but also repeat local clients who liked to enjoy the calming atmosphere, the good food.

It was to be a destination.

And no matter my involvement, she'd do it on her own terms. I was only along for the ride.

Lena's independence astounded me. Despite the lack of support from her parents, the fact that this was a giant undertaking, a huge risk, she forged ahead.

For me, it was an investment. For her, it was a dream.

"Right, Conner?"

I hadn't heard what Lena asked. "Oh, sure."

They shared a look, and both started laughing.

"Glad to know you're paying attention, boy." My grandfather pushed his chair back and stood. "I'll let you kids finish up." He patted my shoulder. "Lunch is on you, grandson of mine. Lena, it has been a pleasure. Tell your grandmother I said hello."

"I will." She watched him go, a sad look in her eyes.

"What's wrong?" I had to know anything that was bothering her, and I wasn't quite sure why.

"It's just sad. They were such good friends and drifted apart."

"You're thinking about Carter?" I hated how much that bothered me.

"Yes. And no. Also my grandmother. I don't know, Conner, the idea just makes me sad."

The bell over the door rang, and Carter strolled in, his eyes finding us immediately. Chatter followed him as he crossed the diner and slid into our grandfather's vacated seat.

"These anybody's?" Carter pointed to the uneaten plate of cheddar fries.

"Grandfather's." I eyed him, wondering what he was doing there.

"His loss." Carter shrugged and dug in, barely coming up for air as he inhaled the food.

"Uh, Carter." Lena waited for him to lift his eyes. "How'd you find us?"

"Oh." He swallowed a bite. "It's all over social media. This weird lunch that's happening."

"Why would people post about seeing us here?"

Carter stole my milkshake, removed the straw, and downed the rest of it.

"Go ahead," I said. "Apparently, I wasn't drinking that."

Carter flashed me a grin. "Thanks, bro. And to answer your question, Lena, it's because the *Weekly Wine* can't get an issue out fast enough to spread the news. You know, it's really like spotting a unicorn. Definitely news worthy."

"What news?" Lena met my gaze.

Carter focused on the fries in front of him as he said, "This weird friendship you guys have now. It's not supposed to happen, you know. That's why you're a unicorn. No one thought you could ever be friends."

"We aren't friends," Lena was quick to say.

"Definitely not." I sent her a nod in solidarity.

Carter shrugged. "Could have fooled me. Neither of you are particularly friendly, and the pictures on social are all smiley."

"Pictures?" I rubbed my forehead.

Carter pulled out his phone and tapped the social icon, pulling up the group that was just for residents of Superiore Bay. "You even have a ship name."

Lena and I both leaned in for a better look. There was a picture of the two of us, my grandfather conveniently cut out. We were laughing about something, and it used the hashtag Selennor. "Selennor?"

Carter slid his phone back into his pocket. "Don't worry, we'll come up with a better name."

Lena groaned and rested her head on her arms. "Seriously, can this town get any nosier?"

"I wouldn't ask that." Carter's entire body shook with laughter. He was enjoying this.

"Why not?" I wasn't sure I wanted to know.

"Because the answer to that question in Superiore Bay is yes, we can always get weirder."

Selennor. The name was awful, but I wasn't sure the friendship we both denied would be.

Chapter Twenty-Seven
LENA

I studied the drawings just like the lead architect told me to.

And now, I was freaking out.

Full-on, I can't do this, freak out.

My hands shook as I tried to take a deep breath to calm myself. They were just drawings. Not brick and stone. We could still scale it back. A lot. I paced to the tiny bunkhouse kitchen to pour myself another cup of coffee.

It was just too much, more than I could handle on my own. What was I even thinking when I dreamed this place up?

Dreaming. That was what I was doing. I flipped to the last page of the construction documents and shook my head. I didn't recognize these buildings. They served no purpose that I could name. I went back to the first page and studied the plans again.

Did we really even need a bed and breakfast? Wouldn't that take business away from the other local B&Bs? I just wanted to create a destination. A year-round experience where people could come apple picking in the fall, maybe do a little shopping in the general store and take a hayride with their kids. And in winter, they could come ice skating, pick out a Christmas tree, and sip hot chocolate and apple cider. In the spring and summer, my place would be where people went when the beach was too crowded, or when the rain brought everyone into town for shopping. It didn't need to be anything more than that.

I rolled up the set of documents and put them back in the tube. Grabbing my keys and my travel mug, I headed out the door before I could second guess myself.

Grams didn't like it when I rode my moped at night, but this was important. I had to talk to my partner before things went any further. There was me being scared and cautious, and then there was me being smart and cautious. I wanted to be the latter.

My old moped started to shake just as I reached the apex of the enormous bridge that stretched across the bay. I could always count on her to get me to the top, but it was always touch and go there for a minute or two. I eased her down the other side at a slow pace to give her a break.

Even in the darkness of the late hour, I could still see Ashford Estates sitting high along the cliffs opposite the bay. It occurred to me then that I had no idea how I would find Conner on such a big estate. Did he live in the house with his father? Or did he have a place somewhere on the grounds?

Anyone in Superiore Bay knew where the gates to the Ashford Estates were located, but few had been inside those gates—at least few of the sort of people I knew.

I paused at the base of the bridge, pulling to the side of the road.

Lena: I need to talk to you. I'm coming over, but how do I get past your gigantic golden gates?

Conner: Are they gold? I never noticed. The guest passcode is 091421. Come find me in the barn near the house, you'll see my car.

Lena: Be there in five.

Conner: Okay, but stop freaking out before you get here.

"I am not freaking out." I pushed my moped back onto the street and made a right at the light to head up Oceanside Drive. "It's called being practical, you over-privileged brat." My moped sputtered and skipped as I coaxed her up the hill to the gated entrance of the estate. I really hoped there weren't any more hills between here and the barn.

"Ha! They are gold." I pulled up to the high gates, leaning over to punch the code into the box, but it was all digital and sophisticated.

"Access denied," the AI voice said.

"Come on, what do you want from me?" I muttered as I parked and leaned over the box.

"Oh, you want a face scan? Really?" I rolled my eyes and looked down at the sleek looking box, making a face at it. "What, you Ashfords think this is the Pentagon or something?"

"One moment while I check with the family." The voice sounded like something straight out of a movie where artificial intelligence took over the world.

"Please say your personal code. Mr. Conner Ashford is expecting you."

I scowled and rattled off the numbers Conner had given me.

"Thank you, you will be greeted shortly. Please proceed to the barn, and do not wander the property unescorted."

"What the actual heck?" I muttered as the gates finally opened. I zoomed through them before Ms. Smarty Pants AI could decide I wasn't fancy enough to come inside these gates.

The tree-lined drive was beautiful in the moonlight. To my

surprise, it wasn't overly landscaped. The Ashfords had let the rows of giant red maple trees flourish from generations past. It was lovely in the moonlight. Calming even.

I slowed as the long drive led me through the tunnel of trees, taking a deep breath to get my head on straight. I had legitimate concerns about these plans. I just needed to keep my conversations with Conner focused and not let him shove my issues aside like they were nothing.

Moonlight flooded the immaculate lawn beyond the tree-lined drive. I searched for the barn, seeing nothing but the enormous mansion lit up like the fourth of July.

Then, I saw it. It was the fanciest barn I'd ever seen. It looked more like a brick house than a place to keep a few horses. Isolated from the house, it stood nestled in a copse of birch trees. Built of white brick with a steep red tiled roof and exposed beam trusses, it was … adorable. Like the stables at a fairytale castle. There was even a turret.

"Only on the Ashford Estate." I rolled my eyes and parked my old moped beside Conner's sports car. The *barn* even had a paved parking lot and red brick steps that led up to the open barn doors.

Duke came out to greet me, his tongue lolling out the side of his mouth as he skidded to a stop beside me and danced around in circles.

"Hey, buddy." I scratched behind his ears. "Where's your dad?"

Duke gave a loud bark and darted back up the steps, glancing behind to make sure I followed.

I grabbed my tube of architectural drawings and my coffee mug and followed the gentle giant. I was perfectly calm and rational. We just needed to scale back on my plans.

"Conner?" I called for him as I stepped inside, where it resembled a barn far more than the exterior had. Fresh straw filled the empty stalls at the front of the building, but they were all empty. "Conner?"

I turned a corner and was startled to find an office. A really nice office with a huge oak desk and beautiful lighting and seating. It looked like something out of an interior design magazine.

Duke wrestled in the corner with a huge teddy bear missing an eye and quite a bit of its stuffing.

"Lena?" Conner called from a room behind his office. "In here!"

I followed the sound of his voice into a room filled with really old-looking wine-making equipment. Aged barrels, vintage wooden wine presses and stills. "What is all of this?" I turned around in a circle. "And where are you?" I wandered through a maze of wine casks until I found him at the center of the mess, examining the contents of a barrel of grapes.

"This is my wine room." Conner didn't spare me a glance. "One second and you can freak out."

I folded my arms across my chest. "I am not freaking out."

I watched as he studied his grapes, casting out ones he seemed dissatisfied with, though they looked perfectly fine to me. I drifted to his side, peering into the barrel of the vintage wine press he was using. It smelled funny.

I reached for one of his discarded grapes, but he smacked my hand away.

"Hey!" I rubbed my hand. "What was that for?"

"Don't eat those, they're rubbish."

"Rubbish?" I arched a brow at him, but he didn't answer me. I studied him in his grubby t-shirt and worn jeans. I'd never seen him so … focused.

He set the old press to do its thing, pressing the grapes the old fashioned way, churning and beating the grapes to a pulp with a heavy stone stained with juice.

"Come with me." He grabbed my hand and led me to yet

another room.

This one was filled with small wooden casks and dozens of dusty bottles on racks.

"How much coffee have you had to drink tonight?" Conner perused the shelves of bottles.

"Two or three ... pots," I admitted.

"Hence, the freak out?" He smirked at me, lifting a bottle from its place on the shelf.

"I am not freaking out," I said calmly.

"Have you looked in a mirror lately?" Conner moved to a table covered in the makings of a barrel.

Did he make them himself? I wondered, watching him open the bottle of wine.

"Come, we have to let it breathe for a few minutes." He guided me back to his office and sat me down in front of his desk.

"You have a sticky note stuck to your forehead." He leaned back in his chair.

"What?" I touched my forehead, and sure enough, my fingers came away with one of those small, square sticky notes in bright pink. Ignoring his chuckle, I tucked it into my pocket. It was one of many notes I'd stuck to the drawings. "Whatever." I shook my head. "We need to talk about scaling back this monstrosity." I waved the tube of drawings at him.

"Monstrosity?" Conner wiped his hands on a towel.

"It's too much." I rolled the drawings out in front of him. "I know you want to go right to phase four, and that's fine, but we need to scale back. Just because you have more money than Midas doesn't mean we need to build a theme park." I shook my head, standing and pacing in front of his desk.

"Theme park? I wasn't aware we'd escalated to apple-themed Ferris wheels and roller coasters." Conner bent his head to study the drawings with my notes. There were a lot of sticky notes.

"We don't need a bed and breakfast. Or the chapel. And I think the current location of the orchard is a mistake."

"Okay." Conner nodded. "Why don't you tell me what you're worried about, and then we can work on a plan to scale things back a bit." He leaned back again and put his feet up on his desk.

I sat down in the leather chair opposite him. "What if we aren't as successful as everyone thinks we'll be? What then? We go straight to phase four with things we might not need yet, and then what happens if we struggle to get this business off the ground? Then, we're stuck with buildings we didn't need that we can't afford to keep open."

"I see. A valid worry." Conner nodded.

"I mean, Conner, there are buildings in these plans that I don't even know what they're for. I just think we'd be smart to trim some of the excess."

"Hold that thought." Conner stood. "I'll be right back, but find whatever you're not sure about, and we'll make sure we discuss it with the architects."

I moved behind his desk to flip through the documents to find the pages with the rows of shops I didn't remember discussing. There were at least twelve shops I had zero plans for, and a few of them looked like they had two stories.

"Taste this." Conner came up behind me with two glasses of amber-colored wine. His arm wrapped around to my front, cupping the glass of wine in his hand.

I took the glass and pointed to the pages laid out on his desk. "We don't need any of this."

"Lena, sit and drink your wine. I need an opinion." Conner pointed to my seat.

I moved to the chair and sipped the wine. "It's good." I set it down, turning back to the drawings.

"Good?" Conner leaned forward. "Good?"

"Tasty," I offered.

"Try it again and focus on what you're doing, Lena. One does not merely sip a fragrant hybrid wine and say it's good. You need to experience the wine."

"Experience it?" I rolled my eyes. It was wine, for crying out loud.

"That's it." He stood up. "Sit back." He ordered.

"Fine." I sat back against the soft leather seat.

"Put your feet up." He scooted a low footstool out from under his desk, and I humored him.

"Now, close your eyes and take three deep, cleansing breaths. In and out, slowly."

"What, are we meditating now?" I scowled up at him.

"No scowling permitted while we are tasting wine. Wine tasting is supposed to be fun."

"Wine tasting is fun when you don't have a million other things on your mind."

"Do you even know how to relax?" Conner laughed at me, and I couldn't help but return his smile. I liked this version of him, the one he'd probably never have let me see outside this office.

"Fine, I will taste the wine." I started to take another sip.

"Start with the fragrance first," Conner instructed.

"I have to smell it?"

"Yes, that is part of the experience."

"Rich people are so weird." I sighed into my glass, inhaling the scent. "Oh, that's nice," I hummed, taking another whiff. "What is that, apple blossoms?"

"Yes." I could practically hear Conner's grin. "But it's not really apple wine, per se."

I took a careful sip, letting the wine run over my taste buds. There was a distinct floral taste, but with a hint of pear and apple notes in addition to the underlying grape flavors.

"This is really good, Conner." I took another sip. "We should totally serve this at the restaurant."

"My thoughts exactly. We should only serve it at the restaurant and nowhere else."

"I love that idea. It's perfect without being too appley." I lifted my glass for a refill. "Did you make this yourself?" I gestured at the room behind his office.

Conner nodded. "I started working with the apple blossoms right around the time we got serious about this partnership. It's not perfect yet, but it will be in time for our big restaurant opening. Unless, of course, you think we need to cut that too." He gave me a mischievous smirk.

"No, the restaurant is a must. But I'm serious about all this other stuff." I pointed to the drawings on his desk.

"This is what set you off tonight?" Conner ran a hand across the pages.

"I don't even remember talking about these buildings."

"That's because we didn't. I asked the architects to include plenty of commercial space." He leaned forward to refill my glass.

"We already have plenty of commercial space," I protested.

"For your plans, yes. We have allotted a space for each of your shops and event spaces, but this is for back up."

"Back up?" I took another sip of the most perfect wine I'd ever tasted.

"Just in case our business struggles to get off the ground."

"How are a bunch of empty stores supposed to help us if that happens?" I was growing impatient.

"Well, on the off chance that we need the extra income, we can lease these shops to other store owners. That will increase our monthly revenue to help us through any difficult times."

"Wait. What?" I leaned over the drawings.

"Commercial property is a good investment, Lena. It's good to have the space for our own growth and also for others to come join us and benefit from our success."

"Okay. I didn't know that." I felt a little foolish for coming all the way over here in a freak out.

"Should we discuss the inn? If you'd like to scale back at all, I agree that is probably the best place to do it."

"I don't know." I leaned against his desk, putting my head down on my arms. "I'm so confused. It all just feels too big. Like we've thrown everything into this but the kitchen sink. Did you see where they added a park with a carousel?" I flipped to the third page of the documents.

"Of course they added things. That's what architects do. It's like they can't help themselves." Conner sipped his wine, swishing it in his mouth before he scribbled something in a notebook.

"We need to take that out, though ..." I stuttered, trying not to say what I was going to say.

"Though, what?"

"The carousel would be so pretty. But it's definitely got to go."

"Along with the inn?" he asked. He was going to leave it to me to make this decision.

"Is it necessary? Aren't we just taking business away from the other B&Bs in town?"

"Wait. Let me get this straight." Conner chuckled. "You're not worried *about* the competition. You're worried *for* the competition?"

"Well, yes." I frowned at him. "I don't want to put anyone out of business."

"That's why we made it cozy and small." He turned the pages to the drawings of the inn. "It's only sixteen rooms. It will stay booked that way, and it won't take business away from your competitors. At least not too much."

"So, what you're saying is, I'm pretty much overreacting again, right?" I put my feet up on the desk and lifted my wine glass toward his. "Probably won't be the last time."

Chapter Twenty-Eight

CONNER

"I have another wine for you to test before I call a car to take you home." I grabbed the empty bottle and went to retrieve the second one. I hoped she liked it as much as I did.

"I drove here." Lena frowned at me.

"That thing you ride is hardly more than a bicycle, I'm not even sure how you made it all the way here."

"It was touch and go." She giggled, and I liked the sound of it. I wondered what it might be like to be the one to make her laugh every day.

"Besides, we've put away a whole bottle of wine already. Neither of us should be doing any driving tonight." I stepped into my wine cellar and grabbed the test bottle. I'd opened it earlier to let it breathe longer.

"My grams would say that makes you a gentleman, but I'm not so sure she has the best judgment. She's kind of cagey, my grams."

"And you're a little drunk." I set the dusty bottle of wine on my desk between us, shaking my head at Duke, who was curled up beside her with his head on her lap. "You sorry traitor." I laughed. "I think my dog likes you better than he likes me."

"He's got good taste." Lena brushed her fingers through his fur, and I could swear his eyes literally rolled back in his head.

"You may regret spoiling him. He's a big baby, and he's pushy when it comes to head scratches and belly rubs."

"He can have all he wants of both." Lena leaned down and kissed him on the head. And just like that, I was jealous of my dog. I poured another round and handed her the glass.

"I don't drink much so I'm a light weight. I don't usually even like wine, but that first one was really good." She reached for her glass, and our fingertips brushed for a brief moment. Despite the urge to curl my hand around hers, I yanked it back.

"Then, this should knock your socks off." I swirled the deep red wine in my glass, trying not to look up into her gorgeous eyes.

"It's pretty." She studied the rich wine before she inhaled the bouquet, an adorable crease of concentration forming between her brows. "And spicy."

"Mulled wine. I thought it would be an excellent holiday-only, private label for purchase in our finest store."

"I love that idea." She breathed in the fragrance like I showed her with the last bottle. "Oh, that smells like Christmas." She took a careful sip. "I taste cinnamon and nutmeg." She took another sip. "Allspice and something more savory with a bit of a bite."

"Cardamom and orange zest, with hint of apple blossom." For a reason I couldn't begin to unravel, I wanted her to like my wine, needed her to.

"It's delicious but not overpowering. I've never had mulled wine. I always thought it would be too spicy, but this is lovely." She swirled the contents of her glass and took another sip. "I could get used to this."

"The secret is adding the mulling spices early in the process so they don't overpower the wine but complement it."

"Well done." She lifted her glass with a smile, meeting my

gaze. "My mom will be our best customer. She's going to love this stuff."

"I have several bottles, you should take her one."

"Oh, she's not ready for that yet." Lena laughed, but her face pinched in sadness. "She still doesn't like this whole partnership thing."

"I'm sorry for that. I hate to be the source of any ... tension within your family."

"She'll come around once she sees the results. Once she sees my plans are actually moving forward." Lena let her hands fall back into her lap, and Duke was quick to nudge her to work on his ears.

"And your father?" I couldn't imagine how he must have reacted to our partnership.

"Dad is ... reserved." Lena sat quietly in her chair, staring over my shoulder. "He is never quick to give an opinion until he sees the big picture. He doesn't like you very much." She gave me an apologetic smile. "But he will respect what we are trying to build together. He just will never want to be beholden to an Ashford for our family's success."

"Sounds a lot like my dad." I was familiar with the type. Quiet. Stern and unforgiving.

"Oh, not at all. My dad's a big old softy when it really matters." Fondness entered her gaze. "I'll talk to him again before we break ground and convince him this is the right move for us. Even if he never agrees with me, he will support me. That's what dads are for anyway."

I was definitely not familiar with that type of father.

"I remember when we were little, Dad was always so excited for the first big snow. It didn't matter if it was the middle of the night or during the school day. Once the ground was covered, he'd come get me and Enzo to play in the snow for hours. He was like a kid himself. We'd go sledding and have snow ball fights, build snowmen. It was always the best day."

"It's no wonder you wanted to create a winter wonderland for kids to experience the magic of the holidays." I smiled into my wine glass, trying to hide my jealousy. I'd never known what it was like to have a father like that, and I never would.

"Maybe. If my—*our* extension of Orchard Hill can bring that kind of magic to other families, then my job is done, and my dad will be proud."

"It must be nice to be so sure of their support even when they haven't given it."

"I may not have their approval yet, but I'll always have their support, Conner." She reached for my hand, and I saw pity in her eyes. That was one emotion I never wanted to see from her.

Maybe it was the wine, or maybe it was the fact that I couldn't get her out of my head—couldn't get the idea of her and Carter out of my head, and that left me feeling irrationally jealous. But I leaned forward, closing the distance between us.

The moment my lips brushed hers, something within me shifted. I wanted more. Reaching to cup her face, I let my fingers slide through her silky hair.

She let out a breath in surprise. She had no idea what she did to me, how much she made me want to be better than I was.

"Conner, no." She pushed against my chest, shaking her head. "We can't."

"Why not?" I blurted. "Ever since that day you pushed me into the bay, I haven't been able to get you off my mind, Selena." I reached for her hand, hoping we could find the easy intimacy we'd shared over the last few hours.

"Is that why you invested?" Anger sparked in her dark eyes, and I knew I had to lay it all on the line.

"No." I leaned back in my chair, scooting away from her to give her some space. "I invested in an amazing woman with an incredible plan and a brilliant mind for business. I invested because this town needs you and your fire and creativity."

"That sounds like a lot of waffle." She frowned at me.

"I'm serious, Lena." I smiled, trying to reassure her. "You deserve a chance to make Orchard Hill Farms one of the premier businesses in this region. You will succeed at anything you set your mind to. As Conner Ashford, the businessman, I want to be part of that." I propped my elbows on the desk between us. "Conner, the guy, though, he likes your fire and the way you stand up for yourself and your family, despite all my family has done to keep you down. I didn't ..." I pushed a frustrated hand through my hair. "This is a surprise to me just as much as it is to you."

"What am I supposed to do with that, Conner?" Her warm brown eyes reflected the war within. The same war I was fighting and losing within myself. We were in business together, and even that was a bridge too far for our families. There was no way this could end well.

"I used to want to avoid you at all costs. I even convinced myself I didn't like you or your family. Now, I can't imagine not being part of this venture with you. I believe in you, Selena Contreras. You have a passion for your work, and that's something I've not had in a long time ... if ever."

"What about your chemistry set?" She quirked a half-smile at me, and I fought the urge to lean forward and feel that smile against my lips.

"It's a hobby." I sighed, hearing my father's disappointed voice in my head. "My little experiments have never really impressed my father."

"I don't understand." Selena's eyes smoldered with purpose. "It means something to you, and you're obviously good at it. If he doesn't see that, fine, whatever, but you shouldn't let it stop you from doing something that brings you joy."

"See, there's that inspiring spirit I admire." I lifted my glass to hers. "You know, it's really annoying sometimes."

"Because I'm right." She offered me a soft smile. "Get used to it." She lifted her glass to tap mine, and I knew we'd turned a corner tonight. Maybe not the one I wanted, but it was still an important step for us either way.

Chapter Twenty-Nine

LENA

"Mark, these look wonderful." I ran my hand over the landscape plan that was so much more than I would have ever dreamed up on my own. "You guys have really brought this place to life." I couldn't stop smiling. I could almost see it now. The rolling hills and forests bordering the new orchard. The quaint little general store where it would all begin. It was happening.

"We still have a long way to go, Lena, but we're going to be ready to break ground soon." Mark returned my smile. He was enjoying this as much as I was.

"Oh, I don't know." I leaned back in my chair in his conference room, gazing at the drawings of the Orchard Hill Farm expansion pinned to walls like paintings in a gallery. "We still have so much to plan before we're ready for that."

"I have something to show you." Mark grinned and turned toward the huge television hanging on the wall.

With the flick of a button on a remote, my dream filled the screen in full scale, three-dimension. I stood up to get a closer look as Mark zoomed in on the general store, sitting nestled among a copse of mature red maples. There were so many wonderful mature trees on the property, we'd all agreed we had to incorporate them into the design.

A cobble-stone walkway led from the store down to the lake, where there was a dock and a gazebo. The landscape design was simple for the moment, but I could already visualize where future stores and restaurants would go.

Mark came to stand beside me. "As we finalize each building, we will fill in this model so you can see it before we ever lay a single brick."

"It's perfect. I can't believe you did this just to help me visualize it."

"It occurred to me the other day that part of your concerns were with not being able to imagine what these flat drawings would actually look like."

"This makes it real, Mark."

He crossed his arms over his chest and turned to me. "So, when we are only looking at the general store and the landscaping, and we forget about all that other stuff that's still in planning mode, how do you feel about breaking ground in two weeks?"

"So soon?" I gaped at him. "What about the contractor we decided on? There's no way she'll have room in her schedule so soon." I really wanted to work with Jenny. She wasn't just a contractor but an interior designer too. She was perfect for this job.

"I talked to Jenny unofficially the other day. Just to see what her schedule was like. We showed her everything, and she wants to be part of this project. She's rearranged her schedule to accommodate these initial plans. We won't be able to get started on the remainder for a few months yet, but I think you're going to be super busy getting the general store open and staffed before the harvest season."

"That would be amazing. You really think we could be open by then?"

"Absolutely."

"But what about the interior plans?" I looked at the general store. The exterior was perfect. We'd spent hours looking at brick and exterior cladding and roofing materials to arrive at the aesthetic. But we hadn't even discussed the inside aesthetic.

"Want to take a tour?" He grinned at me and picked up his remote. And with another click, we were inside the building.

"Shut up!" I sat down, staring at the beautiful interior of the store, filled with shelves and cute little boutique areas around a central retail station where the cashiers would work. There was even a small cafe that would serve as a temporary bakery for now and a future coffee shop later.

Mark guided me through the store so I could see the lighting features, the beautiful hardwood flooring, and barn sliding doors. He led me up the stairs to an area that would serve as storage for now, and a flex-space for the store as it grew over the years. At the back of the building was my office.

I got teary just looking at it. A wall of bookshelves stood behind a huge antique desk and large windows faced what would be the new orchard. I would get to watch it grow and mature right from my office.

"It's beautiful, Mark."

"We can discuss any changes you might want," he began, but I shook my head.

"Really, it's perfect. I can't think of a single thing I would want to change."

"How do you feel about breaking ground now?" Mark elbowed me playfully. I loved working with someone who not only saw my vision too but was just as excited about it as I was.

"Let's do it!" I clapped my hands, refusing to let myself freak out about such a big decision.

"You know, it's customary for large projects like this one

that will impact a community, the way yours will, to have a ground-breaking ceremony. A big to-do to help the whole town feel like they're part of it. It can really amp up anticipation for your store too."

It was on the tip of my tongue to say I couldn't afford something like that. I was so used to having limited funds, the idea of putting on a party for all of Superiore Bay seemed like an impossible feat. But my loans had come through. I now had access to more money than I'd ever seen.

It made me nervous in some ways. That I owed so much to Conner Ashford. But at the same time, it made me more confident about what I was doing.

"I think we could arrange something fun for ground-breaking day."

"I'll schedule it with Jenny, and you and Conner take care of the party."

"Deal." I reached to shake his hand. "Though, I feel like the party is more to keep me out of your hair than anything else." I smirked at him.

"I would never," he deadpanned, walking me to the door.

I strolled down the sidewalk in my best dress and styled hair, feeling like a real grown up for the first time in my life. Like a professional. I could get used to the feeling. If only my family could get on board with my partnership with Conner. If only I could convince myself the partnership was all I wanted from him.

I drove down the dusty drive to the house, hoping Enzo wouldn't kill me for keeping his truck for most of the afternoon. I was going to need to get my own car soon. I couldn't keep riding my moped around town.

"What the actual heck does he think he's doing." I ground to a halt at the back door, where Conner and my father were talking animatedly. They were laughing.

"Lena, you can't keep my truck all day." Enzo charged across the yard from the barn. "I'm late getting to the south fields to meet with the fertilizer guy."

"Sorry." I tossed the keys to him, not taking my eyes off Conner and my dad. Now, they were shaking hands, and even Grams had come out to say goodbye.

Duke sat beside his dad until he saw me and came charging in my direction. I reached out a hand to greet him, distracted by all the camaraderie I wasn't used to seeing between the Ashfords and my family.

They were all smiling and nodding. It was everything I wanted, so why did I feel a gnawing rise of anger in the pit of my stomach?

"Conner." I crossed my arms over my chest as if to protect myself. "I see you've been making friends."

Some of the color drained from his face as his smile faded.

"I thought you had a meeting you couldn't get out of today. That was why you needed me to take the meeting with Mark."

"You didn't really need me for that." He shrugged, trying to brush it off like he hadn't lied about where he had to be today.

He'd meddled into my issues with my family. He'd overstepped. "I don't need you for most things," I spat. Really, I'd just needed his money, his land, and the town support the Ashford name would bring to my expansion of Orchard Hill. Other than that, I didn't need or want anything from him, and it was time he realized that. It was time *I* realized that.

"Lena, I—"

"I think you should leave, Conner." I pointed to his fancy sports car.

"Fine." He threw his hands up in the air, and Duke whined, looking from his dad to me.

"Let's go, Duke," Conner called to his dog, and Duke gave

me a final whine before he darted across the drive to hop into the backseat of the tiny car that was way too small for the dog.

"*Mija?*" Gram came up behind me as I watched the dust fade after Conner left. "He meant well."

"I know." I sighed. "But he can't just stick his big nose into my family life. It's my job to make Mom and Dad comfortable with the idea of my partnership with Conner. I don't need him swooping in like a white knight to make it all better."

"That's not what he did, *Mija*." She moved back to the porch to sit on the swing, patting the place beside her.

"So, what did he do?" I reluctantly sat down on the swing.

"For starters, he brought his special wine you plan to serve in the restaurant and the store. And he also brought copies of your partnership agreement to show your parents what lengths you've taken to protect the family and your father's shares of Orchard Hill. And then, he told us he wanted our blessing on his partnership with you, but only once we've asked you to show us your plans for the Orchard Hill expansion." She paused. "He believes in you. He made that clear."

"He did that?" I immediately felt horrible for what I said to him.

"He wasn't here to fix all your problems for you, *Mija*. He was here because he doesn't want to be responsible for causing trouble within our family. He was being a partner. A good one."

"Still, he shouldn't have gone behind my back to come here."

"Would you have let him?"

"No, probably not."

"The boy cares about you, Lena." Grams took my hand in her weathered one.

"Well, I don't know about that, Grams." I laughed, trying not to think about the kiss from a few nights ago.

"You're an independent young woman, and I'm proud of you. There is nothing wrong with letting your business partner be your partner. He is in this with you. Letting him do his job doesn't make you any less capable."

"I know." I sighed. "You're probably right."

"I know I am." She chuckled softly.

"Any more of that wine?"

"You're not much of a wine drinker, Lena. I think you should let me have it." She gave me a cheeky grin.

"No way, Grams, that's good stuff."

"I'll fight you for it." Grams shot out of the swing like she was twenty and towed me into the kitchen, where Mom was serving a late lunch.

"Lena, come sit." Dad pulled out the chair beside him. "I think it's time you tell us all about your fancy plans. When is it happening, how is it happening, are you sure about it?" He fired his questions quickly, like he'd been holding them back for a long time.

"Well." I smiled as I took my seat. "We are breaking ground in two weeks, and there's going to be a big party."

"So soon?" Mom set a salad on the table and turned back into the kitchen for her famous tamales. "Will you be ready?"

"For the ground breaking, yes. I have some beautiful plans to show you. But for the party, not so much. I'll need your help, Mama. You too, Grams."

"Of course. We'll make a plan tonight." Mom moved to sit beside Dad. "I want to see those drawings again and give them proper time. I don't think any of us realized how serious you've been about all of this, Lena. I hope you know, even when we're uncertain and nervous about your ventures, we will always support you."

"I know that, Mama." I reached across the table to squeeze her hand.

"Are those the drawings?" Dad eyed the roll of paper sticking out of the top of my bag I hooked over the back of my chair.

I grabbed them and laid them flat across the table, my nerves hitting an all-time high. I wanted them to love the expansion as much as I did. "Now, this is just the initial plan for the general store and the landscaping. I'll show you the rest after lunch."

I smoothed a hand across the paper holding my dream.

"Oh, this is lovely," Mom murmured as Dad searched his pocket for his reading glasses. "I'm sorry we didn't look closely before."

"What's this?" Dad zeroed in on the site for the new orchard.

"That is going to be a small apple-picking orchard."

"We'll need to get saplings into the ground as soon as possible." He peered through his lenses.

"You think it's big enough for families to come in the harvest season to pick apples?"

Dad nodded. "I like it, Selena. It will keep them out of my orchard at the busiest time of the year." He gave me one of his mischievous smiles.

"You know very well it'll be a few years before the new orchard is mature enough, so I'm setting up hayrides to bring people up to the south field for apple picking until the expansion is ready."

"I see." Dad nodded again, giving me the side eye.

"Dad, I'm going to pay you for the use of the south orchard." I rolled my eyes.

"You know." Dad took his glasses off and turned to me with a serious expression. And my dad was rarely serious. "I often wondered why Papa left his shares to you. I never questioned it. I knew he had his reasons. I see why now." He shook his head.

"I'm proud of you, Selena. My papa knew you would have the drive and the bravery to take Orchard Hill Farms into the future. He knew you were a sheer force of nature and nothing would stop you. And I know you love Orchard Hill Farm as much as I do." He ran a hand over the drawings. "It is in your blood, and I can't wait to see what happens next."

"I still need you, Dad." I reached for his hand, realizing in that moment how uncertain he must have been about my plans and how he would fit into them. Dad had a lot of years left to give Orchard Hill. It was in his blood too. "I can't do this without you and your endless well of advice and support."

"You will always have that, Selena. Always."

"And Conner? The partnership."

Mom sighed. "I think we were just worried you would be too trusting."

I laughed at that. "I think Conner would disagree with you there. I've driven him insane with all my caveats and what if scenarios."

"You hammered out one heck of a partnership agreement." Dad nodded. "I still don't know if I can trust him, but I trust you, Selena. And you've done everything within your power to protect your assets."

"So … does that mean we have your blessing?"

"You have it and then some." Dad gave me his ornery smile and leaned over the drawings. "So, where is my retirement home going to be?"

Warmth bloomed in me. I hadn't realized how much it wore on me not to have my parents' support, how much it dampened my excitement. But he'd seen it. Conner had known exactly what I needed. How?

How did he understand me when I hardly understood myself?

Chapter Thirty

LENA

"Stupid piece of crap, let's go." I urged my not-so-trusty moped forward, willing her to make it to Ashford Estates in one piece. I had to see Conner.

The old girl shook like a bucket of bolts about to explode all over the deserted road. I'd made it over the bridge and almost to the gates when she started to crap out on me. I was barely moving now, wobbling down the street like a six year old on a bike for the first time.

"I'm sorry, girl, I didn't mean it." I rolled to a stop to give her a rest. I could walk the rest of the way. Blowing the hair out of my face, I pushed my moped alongside of me, making my way to the end of the street.

"What in the world are you doing, Lena?" A car rolled up beside me, and Carter gaped at me, shaking his head and trying not to laugh at my predicament.

"Shut up and give me a ride." I steered my moped to the side of the road. "You think she'll be okay out here?"

"Trust me, no one is going to steal your girl. Get in, loser."

"Shut your face." I ducked into the passenger seat of his tiny sports car.

"I take it you're headed to the estate?" His brow lifted in question. "I don't recommend it. I gave it two stars on Yelp."

"Normally, I'd agree, but I need to see your brother. I'm guessing he's at his barn office and not answering his phone."

"If he's not answering your calls, he's with his grapes." Carter pulled away from the sandy shoulder, kicking up dust behind them. "Why haven't you bought yourself a car yet? You have the funds for it now, and it's kind of a necessity with all you have going on these days."

I picked up on the note of hurt in his voice. I hadn't had much time for my best friend lately, and I felt bad. I needed to check in with him more often. "What are you doing tomorrow afternoon?"

Carter turned to me with a huge grin. "Car shopping, I hope?"

"It's a date."

"Yes!" There wasn't much Carter enjoyed more than shopping for a new car. "I think you'd love a cute little Mercedes. Red, of course."

"Slow down, Mr. Trust Fund. I'm not spending business funds on an expensive car. We're going to look for something used. A Chevy maybe."

"Ugh, on second thought, I think I'm busy tomorrow." Carter shot me a dirty look. "A Chevy, she says." He shook his head in disgust.

"Okay, maybe a Nissan or a Toyota. A sedan," I added when his eyes lit up again. "A moderately priced sedan."

"You just don't know how to have fun, Lena." He sighed. "But we'll find you a perfectly reasonable, boring, turd-brown car that will at least not leave you stranded on the side of the road."

"You can choose the color." I nudged him playfully.

"And the sound system?"

"Sure, as long as it's not expensive."

"Deal." Carter turned toward the golden gates of the Ashford Estates and laid his palm on the fancy scanner. The gates opened after scanning his palm print.

"You'd think we were visiting royalty."

"As far as my father is concerned, we are."

"Man has a high opinion of himself, doesn't he?" I frowned as Carter sailed along the tree-lined drive, right past the barn and the enormous estate.

"Where are we going?" I looked behind us, searching for Conner's car. It was parked by the barn. "His car is back that way."

"He's not there." Carter turned down a narrow road that led through the forest areas surrounding the house. "How do you feel about riding a horse?"

"Hard pass. Can't we just drive to wherever he is?"

"Yes, but not in my precious." Carter swerved into a gravel lot beside an adorable white bricked barn, much like the one I'd visited last time I was here. Except this one was twice the size.

"The stables," Carter explained as he stepped out of the car.

"Not riding a horse, Carter." I followed him around the side of the barn to a garage.

"How about a four wheeler?" He pointed to a row of ATVs.

"Um …" I glanced around the display of wealth. So many toys and none of the Ashfords had time for such things. "How about that?" I pointed to a safe-looking vehicle.

"That's the custodian's golf cart, Lena." Carter rolled his eyes.

"Will it get us where we need to go?" I gave him a pleading look. My moped was about as adventurous as I was going to get.

"Yeah." Carter groaned and stepped into the driver's seat. "Let's go."

"Thank you." I slid in beside him and clutched the arm rest.

"Not so fast!" I gripped the seat with my other hand as we shot out of the barn and zoomed down a grassy hill.

"Live a little, Lena." Carter laughed, driving the death cart along a bumpy path over an open field. The house and barns faded quickly behind us.

Acres of vineyards spread out across rolling hills. It was beautiful but also kind of intimidating to witness first-hand how much the Ashfords owned.

"I thought we were going to the vineyard?" I frowned when we turned away from the rows of vines.

"We are, just not that one."

"Oh, of course you have others." I shrank in on myself, second guessing all my worries over the last few weeks. No wonder Conner was always so calm and collected about our partnership. It was small potatoes compared to this empire of his.

"Just Connor's hybrids." Carter shrugged. "Dad makes him keep it far away from the "real" vineyard so it won't taint his precious grapes."

I laughed at that. "Those two aren't at all alike, are they?" I'd always thought of Conner as a carbon copy of *The Ashford*, but the man I'd grown fond of recently was nothing like his abrasive father.

"This place is in Conner's blood in a way it never has been for the rest of us. That's the only similarity they share." Carter glanced at me. "You get that now, right?"

"I do." I nodded. "He's stuck behind his father's shadow."

"But he won't be forever," Carter added. "And that will be a great day for everyone. The day Conner Ashford realizes he's a better man than the one who raised us." Carter turned a corner, and we were driving along a cliff over the ocean.

"You slow your butt down right now, Carter." I clutched the armrest, staring down the rocky slope to the narrow strip of beach below.

"Relax, Lena. I've been driving this road since I was a kid."

"Well, I haven't, so slow down."

"Conner likes his hybrid grapes to breathe the ocean air." Carter pointed to the rows of vines stretching from the cliff to a brick shed across a wide, grassy slope. "Dad insists the salt air kills the sweetness of the grapes. As you can imagine, I've been subjected to some super boring dinner conversations that always turn into heated arguments."

"You sure he's here?" I scanned the rows of grapes that were clustered into groups of different species. I couldn't see Conner anywhere. But as soon as we came to a stop near a small brick shed that was a mini version of the barn I'd first visited, Duke came bounding out to greet us.

"Hey, Duke." I stepped out of the cart to greet my favorite Ashford.

"He's probably lost in his work inside." Carter let out a sharp whistle. "Conner, you have a visitor!"

"Get lost, Carter," Conner called back from the shed. "I'm busy."

"Your visitor is much prettier than me, and that's saying a lot."

"What are you babbling about?" Conner stepped out of his shed, and my jaw almost hit the ground.

I'd always thought Conner was handsome. Who wouldn't? But this Conner was shirtless and sweaty, with grubby old jeans sitting low on his hips. He ran a hand through his sweat-damp hair, and he looked like one of those ripped calendar guys come to life.

"Put your tongue back in your mouth." Carter elbowed me. "That's my brother you're gawking at."

"You can go now, Carter." I stepped forward.

"What am I, a chauffeur?"

"Pretty much," I called over my shoulder. "I'll get a ride back with Conner."

"You realize that's going to be by horseback?" Carter pointed at the black as night stallion grazing nearby.

"Take Ares back with you." Conner reached back into the shed for his t-shirt. "I'll drive Selena back later." He gestured to the golf cart.

"Fine. That horse hates me, though." Carter shot a glare at me and his brother. "And I don't like this … whatever this is." Carter took his time approaching Ares and lifting himself up into the saddle. "If he throws me, and I come up damaged, you're a dead man, Conner."

"Send me the bill." Conner cracked a smile, but he didn't spare a glance for his retreating brother.

"Call me if you need me, Lena. I'm serious." Carter reluctantly left us alone. "Duke, watch our girl," he called over his shoulder and cantered away on Ares.

Duke took his orders seriously and came to lean against me.

"You named your horse Ares, after the god of war?" I asked, hoping to break whatever tension there was between us.

"He has a bad temper. Won't let anyone ride him but me." Conner grinned. "Carter's probably going to end up walking home."

"Why did you do it?" I blurted. But I needed to understand his motives for visiting my family.

"Do what?" He folded his arms across his chest as if to protect himself from whatever onslaught he anticipated.

"Why did you talk to my family behind my back?"

"It wasn't about keeping anything from you. It was just something I needed to do."

"Why, Conner?" I sank my hands into Duke's fur to keep myself steady.

"I didn't see it, Lena. For a long time, I missed it, overlooking you with your crappy mode of transportation, your messy hair and overalls."

"Ouch."

"I was a fool, Lena." He took a step forward. The only thing between us was Duke, who thought this was a pet-Duke party. "I didn't see what kind of powerhouse you were all this time. I didn't see who you were and how amazing you are. I underestimated you in every way … and I didn't want the people you love the most to make that same mistake. I know how much your family means to you, and I knew you'd never be able to make them see you as anything more than their daughter. Like my father will never see me as anything more than the less-than-perfect Ashford heir." He took a step back, shaking his head.

"I know your family doesn't see you like that, but I wanted to show them what they were missing. I didn't do it as your business partner overstepping. I did as your friend who cares."

"I didn't see you either." I finally managed to get a word in. "Not until I saw this place." I turned toward his vineyard. "This is everything you are, Conner Ashford. From the horse, the dog, and the pretentious little building you guys call a shed." I laughed. "And the grapes, and the whole thing about how you want your grapes to breathe the ocean air and your dad thinks that's stupid." I shook my head, not sure if my ramblings made any sense. "You're so much more than I gave you credit for. And I think you've been dealing with that all your life. I'm sorry I didn't see you before, but I see you now." I moved around Duke and stepped into Conner's arms, sliding my fingers into his messy hair. I didn't hesitate as I kissed him. His lips parted in surprise, and his arms wrapped around me.

Epilogue

CONNER

We found Carter walking along the trail back to the vineyards. He was waving his phone in the air, trying to get a signal.

"Need a lift?" Lena teased, scooting closer to my side to make room for Carter.

"Carter?" I frowned at the lost look on his face. I hadn't seen that look in years. Not since Harper Chapman left Superiore Bay and broke his heart. My brother hadn't been the same since.

"You okay?" Lena tried to hand him a bottle of water.

"Yeah, I'm good." He slid in next to her, oblivious of the way she sat with my arm around her shoulders. "Hurry, I need to get back. I'm not getting service out here."

"Carter, you look like you've seen a ghost." Lena glanced up at me with a worried frown. "Did you hit your head?"

He shook his head, staring at his phone on his lap.

I recognized the online chat forum for the *Weekly Wine*.

"Harper is coming back to Superiore Bay. She's recently divorced."

Lena and I shared another worried glance. She knew then.

Any mention of Harper was strictly forbidden, Carter's orders. If she was coming back, it would kill him.

I stepped on the accelerator. Carter needed to get away from Ashford Estates and go wherever he went when he needed a break. Then, it occurred to me that he would want Lena. That was where he went when he needed a friend. I was going to have to learn to share her if we were going to be together, and I was certain that was where this was going. The burn of her kiss was still on my lips, and I wanted nothing more than to show her the surprise I had waiting for her.

"I'll go with you." Lena reached for Carter's hand.

"No. I just need to be alone." And the moment we arrived back at the garage, Carter took off in his car.

"I'm worried." Lena watched him go. "Harper really hurt him when she left. Hurt me too, but not nearly as much."

"He'll be okay." I took her hand, giving it a gentle squeeze. "Give him some time, and then we'll go check on him later."

She turned into my arms, giving me a hesitant smile as she leaned her head against my shoulder. "Thank you for that."

"I have a surprise for you." I tugged on her hand.

"Uh-oh." She followed me around to the front of the main garage bay where we parked the cars. "That's always a little scary."

"My surprises scare you?" I laughed. "How?"

"They usually come with a lot more than I bargained for, but that doesn't mean they're bad," she rushed to add.

I clicked on the garage remote in my pocket and waited for the door to lift, watching her face for her reaction.

"What?" She scowled at me as she looked between me and the BMW parked inside. "Oh, no." She stepped away from me. "Absolutely not. You're not giving me a car, Conner. I'm never going to be that kind of girlfriend."

"Girlfriend?" I closed the distance between us. She stuttered and turned pink. "I like the sound of that, but this isn't a gift from your boyfriend of like the last thirty minutes. It's a company car your partner acquired."

"Acquired?" She arched a brow at me. "As in purchased?"

"I purchased it *used* from one of the vendors we use for the winery, who will also be servicing the Orchard Hill Farms extension. I bought it with our joint operation funds. It's yours to use for business-related driving so they don't see you on that crazy moped." I handed her the keys. "I thought you might like the blue one, but we can look at others if you don't like it."

"It's perfect." She took the keys, wrapping her hand around mine. "I was on board as soon as you said it was used."

"I know you, Selena Contreras. I see you." I pulled her into my arms again. "I won't ever make that mistake again."

"What mistake?" She smiled at me.

"Thinking that a woman capable of pushing me into the bay without a second thought wasn't worth my time. You're worth everything to me now."

Bonus Chapter
HARPER

I belonged in a newsroom. That was what I'd been telling everyone since I was old enough to know what a newsroom was. It was my defense against all the plans my blue blood family tried to make for me, my mother's expectations.

"No, Mom, I won't consider the summer internship with your senator friend because I'm going to be a reporter."

"Dad, you can't force me to sit through a boring dinner listening about the law from your buddy, the defense attorney, because I already knew my path." And it was a respectable one. There were awards to be won in journalism, grand people to meet. If being a Chapman meant anything, it meant being grand.

At least according to most of Boston society.

Somewhere along the way, I fell in love with this job. It became less of a shield and more of the sword I wielded. Maybe I just fell in love with *him*. Garret. I hadn't thought that was possible, that I'd find someone both my parents and I could tolerate. But he was that man.

Was he *the* man? I wasn't so sure.

I leaned back in my desk chair, thanking the heavens I'd

splurged on the ergonomic rolling chair. It had been a long morning chasing a story. Literally chasing it since the story was a Boston politician who refused to answer my questions.

I kicked off my heels and massaged my calves. What I wouldn't do for an iced Boba right about now.

As if conjured from my thoughts, a Thai Tea Boba appeared on my desk. I looked up into the handsome face of my best work friend, Jeffrey—never Jeff. His desk butted up against mine in the bull pen.

"I think I'm in love with you." I sipped the tea and sighed.

Jeffrey's deep laugh reverberated through me. "Should I tell the husband I'm leaving him for *the* Harper Chapman?"

"Oh, absolutely."

He sent me a wink before sliding into his chair. "I did some research for you." He passed a manila folder over the dividing wall.

My eyes widened when I opened it. This was going to save me hours of work. I hadn't been lying when I said I loved this job, but it also tended to take up my entire life. "You're too good to me."

"Someone has to be." I heard the disapproval in his tone. He didn't like my husband. Some days I even agreed with him.

"Give it a rest, okay? Garret isn't even in town right now."

He made a sound in the back of his throat but didn't respond and before long I heard the rapid clacking of his keyboard, telling me he'd disappeared into his work once more. I busied myself flipping through what he'd given me.

A buzzing alerted me to a call and I reached into the purse at my feet for my phone. My grandma's picture appeared, and I smiled. She was my favorite person, and I always wanted to talk to her. But I had so much to do. I slid the phone away and vowed to call her once I called it a night.

She'd understand. She always did.

The call had brought me out of my work, not only because I

loved her more than anyone, but because of where she was calling me from. Superiore Bay. I'd spent summers there until I went to college, and I could honestly say that was the best time of my life.

Opening the bottom drawer of my desk, I pulled out a frame I kept there. It used to sit on my desk, until Garret told me it wasn't professional. In the photo, I was squished between my best friend Lena, and the first boy I'd ever loved, Carter Ashford. We sat with our toes digging into the sand on one of the many beaches at the Corolla Horse Ranch.

Every time I looked at this picture—and there were many— I no longer recognized myself. I'd been a teenager rebelling against my overbearing parents and their upper crust city life-style. All I'd wanted in those years was for Superiore Bay to be my home, for Carter to be my home.

But that was then.

Now, I was a serious journalist, trying to chase worthy stories when my husband—who was also my boss—wasn't saddling me with fluff nothing pieces.

I set the frame back in the drawer, taking care to make sure it was concealed, and shut it. The Boba wouldn't do it. I knew what I needed.

Garret kept a stash of tiny candy bars in his desk. It was the worst kept secret in the entire office. Standing, I gathered myself and wiped all emotion from my face. A call from my grandma shouldn't make me wish for the life I hadn't chosen, the one my parents forced me to leave behind without even a goodbye. The people of Superiore Bay probably hated me for that. I knew Carter would.

"Where are you going?" Jeffrey asked, looking up from where he'd been staring at his screen.

"Just need some chocolate."

He shot to his feet so suddenly it surprised me. "You okay there, big guy?"

"Yeah." A flush crept up his cheeks. "You can't go!"

"What?"

"I mean, let's go out to the store and get some chocolate. I heard Garret was running low."

"He's never running low." I pushed past him. "Stop being weird."

I smiled at my coworkers as I made my way to the steps, but to a person, they averted their eyes. Something was going on.

With a shrug, I climbed the few steps to the walkway that meandered past the main offices where editors wielded their red pens. Metaphorically, of course.

Jeffrey was hot on my heels, but I ignored him, stopping when I found Garret's door cracked open. A crash came from inside and I froze, putting a finger to my lips so Jeffrey would be quiet. If someone had broken into Garret's office, I had to know why.

Reaching out, I pressed a hand against the solid wood door and pushed just enough so it opened slowly.

My world came to a halt, breaks screeched, blood ran cold.

Because there was my supposedly still out of town husband. And the woman kissing him definitely wasn't me.

Jeffrey cleared his throat and the two broke apart. It took Garret a moment to register my presence, but when he stepped forward, I held my hands up. "Harper…"

"I need to…" I could hardly get words out through my rapid breath. "Go. I need to go." Turning on my heel, I raced from the office.

Jeffrey didn't speak until we reached my desk. "You know guys like Garret… straight guys… this is what they do."

He was wrong. I refused to believe all men treated women as if our feelings didn't matter. Because I'd known one who only ever wanted to make me happy.

My phone rang again, and this time my mother's name

appeared. I didn't answer. Of those two women, there was only one I could count on.

"I can't be here, Jeffrey."

"Take some time off, sweetie."

"No, I can't be in Boston." Everything here was tied to my life with Garret, a life it had taken me this long to realize wasn't mine. His betrayal hurt, but it didn't crack my heart. I wasn't so stunned that I didn't realize this *should* break me. But it wouldn't.

And that was a problem, wasn't it?

"Why don't you take some of that vacation time you have piling up? Go to a beach."

I had no one to go to the beach with, and it wasn't what I needed, not when I needed something I couldn't explain. I needed my grandmother, someone who'd love me and not try to fix me, not try to order my life.

It was time to go back to Superiore Bay.

How does the reunion between Carter and Harper go? Find out in the Second Chance. Available at all retailers.

THE SECOND CHANCE

They're exes...
   ...nothing more.

Harper Chapman is running away. From her overbearing parents, and from a husband who broke her heart, a man who also happened to be her boss at one of the most prestigious newspapers in the country.

The job was a dream come true. The husband, not so much.

She just wants to go back to a simpler time when summers at her grandmother's house could fix anything. But going back means facing things better left in the past.

Small town gossip.
   And him. The first boy she ever loved.

Carter Ashford is everything she never wants to remember. Charming, drop-dead gorgeous, and a member of the exclusive Ashford family, practically town royalty. Ten years ago, Harper walked away from Superiore Bay, from him. Now, back in town, she does everything she can to avoid the feelings she's never gotten over.

When she realizes the local newspaper has turned into a gossip rag, Harper knows she can fix it. She can spend her limited time here reviving something that actually matters, and then move on to the next chapter of her life.

But could her return prove to be more than she can handle? Harper might learn the only thing better than running away is finding a reason to stay.

Available at all Retailers.

About Ann Maree

Ann Maree Craven is an Amazon bestselling author of Young Adult Contemporary Fiction and YA Fantasy (her Fantasy fans will know her as Melissa A. Craven). Her books focus on strong female protagonists who aren't always perfect, but they find their inner strength along the way. Ann Maree's novels will appeal to audiences of all ages and fans of almost any genre. She believes in stories that make you think and she loves playing with foreshadowing, leaving clues and hints for the careful reader.

Ann Maree draws inspiration from her background in architecture and interior design to help her with the small details in world building and scene settings. (Her degree in fine art also comes in handy.) She is a diehard introvert with a wicked sense of humor and a tendency for hermit-like behavior. (Seriously, she gets cranky if she has to put on anything other than yoga pants and t-shirts!)

Ann Maree enjoys editing almost as much as she enjoys writing, which makes her an absolute weirdo among her peers. Her favorite pastime is sitting on her porch when the weather is nice with her two dogs, Fynlee and Nahla, reading from her massive TBR pile and dreaming up new stories.

Visit me at Melissaacraven.com for more information about the series and discover exclusive content.

Want to see more books by Ann Maree Craven?

You can find them here.

facebook.com/emergenovel

twitter.com/melissaacraven

instagram.com/melissaacraven

pinterest.com/craven0095

About Michelle

Michelle MacQueen is a USA Today bestselling author of love. Yes, love. Whether it be YA romance, NA romance, or fantasy romance (Under M. Lynn), she loves to make readers swoon.

The great loves of her life to this point are two tiny blond creatures who call her "aunt" and proclaim her books to be "boring books" for their lack of pictures. Yet, somehow, she still manages to love them more than chocolate.

When she's not sharing her inexhaustible wisdom with her niece and nephew, Michelle is usually lounging in her ridiculously large bean bag chair creating worlds and characters that remind her to smile every day - even when a feisty five-year-old is telling her just how much she doesn't know.

Want to see more books by Michelle? You can see them at MichelleLynnAuthor.com

 facebook.com/MichelleMacQueenAuthor

Made in the USA
Columbia, SC
13 May 2024

35233986R00128